Luci

By the same author

The Happy Hooker
Letters to the Happy Hooker
Xaviera!
The Best Part of a Man
Xaviera's Supersex
Xaviera Goes Wild!
Xaviera Meets Marilyn Chambers (with Marilyn Chambers)
Knights in the Garden of Spain
Xaviera's Magic Mushrooms
Madame l'Ambassadrice
The Inner Circle

XAVIERA HOLLANDER

Lucinda, My Lovely

PANTHER
Granada Publishing

Panther Books
Granada Publishing Ltd
8 Grafton Street, London W1X 3LA

Published by Panther Books 1984
Reprinted 1984

First published in Great Britain by
Aiden Ellis Publishing Limited 1983

Copyright © Xaviera Hollander 1983

ISBN 0-586-05786-2

Printed and bound in Great Britain by
Collins, Glasgow

Set in Baskerville

To all my lovers – past, present and future.

Part 1

1

Lucinda was excited. Although she was getting on for sixteen, this would be the first time that she was going on holiday without her family. It was an adventure and she felt very grown-up.

She smiled happily at Jennifer Maxwell as they waited for Jennifer's father to come to the school to collect them. Jennifer was a year older than Lucinda and was already a self-assured young lady. Both girls were pretty, but in very different ways. Jennifer was tall for her age and boyishly slim. She had lustrous black hair, dark eyes and sensitive, mobile features. Lucinda had fluffy golden hair and her figure was more rounded and feminine than that of her companion. Happiness gleamed in her big green eyes and she squeezed Jennifer's hand.

Ever since her first term at Hurstmonbury School, Lucinda had looked up to Jennifer with a mixture of reverence and affection. Jennifer seemed to be so much more accomplished, more able to cope with the world of adults, that Lucinda felt herself to be a mere child. She looked to the older girl for guidance throughout her schooldays and she would go to Jennifer with all her problems, from arithmetic to boy friends. She copied slavishly Jennifer's way of dressing, of walking, of talking as if, by imitating her mannerisms, Lucinda would become more like her idol and, at the same time, give expression to her adoration.

For her part, Jennifer accepted this worship with quiet good humour. Not so long ago, she had also looked up to an older girl as if she were a goddess and so she had a good idea of the passionate attachment that Lucinda had formed for her. Jennifer was always gentle with her but Lucinda felt that she was as remote, as unattainable, as a star in the heavens. So, when Jennifer had invited her to spend a few weeks during the summer holidays with her and her father, Lucinda was overwhelmed and begged her own parents to let her go.

'I suppose it will be all right,' her father assented cautiously. 'You're growing up fast and you can't be tied to your mother's apron strings for ever. Jennifer seems to be a nice, sensible girl and I'm sure that you will be looked after. Off you go and enjoy yourself.'

Both girls were wearing the grey flannel skirt and jacket of the school uniform as they waited in the entrance hall. They had packed a few clothes and toilet things into tiny suitcases.

'Daddy's car is frightfully cramped, so don't bring anything you can do without,' Jennifer had warned. 'When we get home, you can borrow some of my clothes. Anyway, we won't be dressing up or going to any fancy parties. It's just a country cottage – I hope that you won't be too bored, Lucinda.'

'Don't worry, I'm sure that it will be lovely. We'll have a lot of fun together.'

In fact, while Lucinda was ecstatic at the prospect of spending her days with Jennifer, she was rather nervous at meeting her father. Merton Maxwell was a legend. Lucinda had seen plenty of pictures of him, for Merton was one of the most celebrated actors of his day. A great Shakespearean stage star in the tradition of John Gielgud, Laurence Olivier or Alec Guinness, like them he had built up a second career on the screen, film and television. Jennifer had told Lucinda that her father kept a flat in town but that, whenever he had the chance, he loved to get away to relax in his cottage in the Cotswolds.

'There'll just be the three of us – no servants, no other house guests.' Jennifer put her arm around her friend's shoulder. 'Still, there are some beautiful walks and good riding as long as the weather holds. Oh, here's Daddy, now.'

They picked up their cases and hurried out on to the gravel

drive where a blood red Ferrari had just screeched to a halt. Merton leaped out, swept off his check cap and made a deep, highly theatrical bow.

'Ladies,' his rich voice echoed in the still air, 'Your servant!'

'Oh, Daddy, do come off the stage,' Jennifer laughed.

The great actor's pantomime had dispelled Lucinda's shyness and she looked with keen interest at the man who stood before her. Her first impression was that Merton was shorter than she had expected. He was really quite a small, stocky man, but his movements were so well calculated, so deliberate, that he was as lithe and as graceful as a panther. His face was rugged and suntanned, but it had an aristocratic sharpness of features and he carried his forty-five years with a swagger. Lucinda noted that he had the same bold, darting eyes and sensitively shaped nose as his daughter. When he smiled, Merton certainly was impressive: he had presence, yet he was completely approachable. Such was his charm.

'So, you are Lucinda. I've heard a lot about you from Jenny.'

He turned his gaze on Lucinda. She felt that his eyes were looking right through her: it was as if her body and her mind were stripped naked before that penetrating stare. She realized that she was blushing and, for a moment, she was at a loss for words.

'Well, hop in,' Merton called. 'There's not much room for you both and for your baggage, but we won't be too long on the road.'

They bustled about and shortly were stowed into the low sports car; Merton accelerated up the drive and Hurstmonbury was left behind them.

After about twenty minutes, Merton turned off the motorway and they made their way through leafy lanes, past sleepy villages of picturesque half-timbered cottages with thatched roofs and silent churches with tall spires. The warm, homely roadside pubs were the only places which appeared to

11

be busy as they sped past. Near the end of their journey, Lucinda saw a great house, standing in its own parkland, its turrets and gables and mullioned windows dominating all the woods and meadows for miles around.

'Don't get any wrong ideas,' Merton smiled at Lucinda as he followed her gaze, 'our house is not a bit like that. Nor like your own stately home. We live rough.'

They crossed an ancient bridge over a running stream and turned into a narrow driveway. Tall oak trees cast a dappled shade over the twisting path. And there stood Merton's cottage.

After the apologies which the Maxwells had made, Lucinda was expecting to be confronted by a hovel. Instead, she saw a handsome house of the lovely, honey coloured Cotswold stone, with long, old fashioned sash windows and a brightly painted green front door. It might have been a rectory or the home of a well-off country doctor: by no means was it a mere cottage.

Once inside, Lucinda was shown straight to her own room. The house had a pleasant, fresh smell, a sense of being lived in. Lucinda unpacked her things and placed them in the chest of drawers. She turned down the patchwork bedspread and savoured the crisp freshness of the sparkling white sheets and pillow cases. There were a few sprigs of lavender in a china vase on her bedside table and the delicate scent seemed to be welcoming her. She liked her little room and, as she scampered downstairs, she felt at home.

The next few days passed pleasantly enough. For much of the time, Merton left the two girls to amuse themselves. He spent several hours each morning in his study: he was busy learning his part in a new play which was to open in the autumn. Lucinda and Jennifer tidied up the house and went for long walks in the village or through the woods with Sheridan, Merton's boisterous Irish setter, which bounded excitedly around the girls and vainly chased every cat for miles around. In the afternoons, they would play tennis, the 'cottage' had a beautifully tended grass court, or simply sit around and gossip. Merton would entertain them with scandalous stories about Hollywood personalities or the more eccentric members of the British aristocracy who were devotees of the stage. Lucinda suspected that his yarns were highly embellished, if not downright inventions, but that did not in any way diminish her enjoyment of them. Sometimes they would go out for dinner to an old manor house which had been converted into a very high class restaurant about ten miles away. Often, they would stay at home and eat something simple which the girls would throw together. Occasionally, Merton would take over the culinary arrangements and produce for them some remarkable meals, for he was a great lover of good food and a capable and imaginative cook.

Although Lucinda had come to the house in order to be with Jennifer, she found that she was enjoying the company of Merton as much as that of her friend. She felt vaguely guilty, as if she were being disloyal, but she had to admit that Merton was so considerate and such good fun, that it was impossible not to like him.

But her feelings went much further than that. He was never pretentious but she was always conscious of being in the presence of a great actor. For years, she had admired and respected him from afar. She had seen him on the stage and the screen and he had haunted her dreams. He was the prince who, one day, would rescue her from some evil dragon, the knight who would carry her colours into battle for her hand, the sheikh who would steal into her tent beneath the tropical moon. In a word, she was starstruck.

Now that she was living in the same house as Merton, she experienced a new warmth and tenderness towards him. He was a big-hearted, gentle man with his own daughter and he extended the same affection to Lucinda. She felt drawn towards him by an immense attraction which she did not fully understand. Could this be love? She dared not think about it.

A week had gone by. It was one of those days when bright sunshine alternated with cloudy, windy weather. The two girls had gone for a canter in the afternoon: Merton's 'cottage' boasted its own stables.

'You ride well,' Jennifer called to Lucinda, as they followed a narrow path between rows of majestic chestnut trees. 'I suppose you were practically born in the saddle.'

Lucinda laughed. 'I can't remember a time when I could not ride. What a lovely view, let's stop for a few minutes.'

They had emerged into a clearing and, on the far side, the ground fell away in a glorious panorama of woods and meadows and thatched cottages clustered around the peaceful church towers. They tethered their horses to a sapling and stretched their limbs on the long, sweet grass.

'Don't you find that riding does something to you?' Lucinda asked.

'What sort of things?'

'Well, I'm not sure how to say it, but the rubbing of the saddle always excites me. When your legs are wide open and you feel the rough skin of your horse's back pricking through your breeches. It makes you feel – well, sexy?'

Lucinda looked shyly at Jennifer and felt herself blushing.

'I think there's more than you are telling me,' Jennifer replied, taunting the younger girl. 'Was there something in your lurid past, Lucinda? Have you been ravished by a wild horse, or do you lust after a fine steed?'

Both girls giggled.

'Nothing like that, you idiot! But there was something – yet it was truly nothing, nothing at all.'

'Stop making a mystery of it. What happened?'

'It was ages ago,' Lucinda confided, 'and I had my first pony. There was a meeting of the hunt – you know there's one very close to where I live. Daddy was riding to hounds but I was much too young. The hunt assembled outside an old country pub and I went along to see them off. You know what it's like – the splendid scarlet jackets, the hounds yapping like

14

mad, men blowing horns, people taking their last quick drink, their stirrup-cups. And I was so proud of my new pony although she looked tiny against the big hunters. There was one man, his name was Colonel Fortescue, I remember, who was so good-looking. Mind you, he wasn't young. Must have been well into his forties at least and, to me, that was as old as Father Time. But there was something about him. He was tall and had a terrific, bushy moustache and he had huge hands and a loud voice. It doesn't sound anything but he struck me as the most manly man I had ever seen. He was always kind to me: never talked down to me like so many grown-ups.'

'So, what happened?'

'Nothing, Jennifer. I keep telling you, absolutely nothing.'

'There must have been something, otherwise you wouldn't make such a fuss about it.'

'Well, eventually, they all rode off and I watched them until they were out of sight. Then, I decided to go for a short ride on my own. Actually, I went a lot further than I had intended: it was such a lovely day I just didn't notice how far I had gone. I stopped because, well, because I wanted to do a pee.'

'Nothing wrong with that?' smiled Jennifer.

'No, of course not. And there was nobody about, or so I thought. So I climbed down and crouched behind a bush. I was wearing jeans and I had them down around my ankles, when I heard the sound of a horse cantering up. I couldn't get my jeans up properly before I found myself face to face with Colonel Fortescue.'

'Face to face?' Jennifer demanded.

'Well, I was showing a great deal more than my face,' Lucinda admitted.

'What did the dashing colonel do? Don't tell me that a gallant English soldier took unfair advantage of a damsel in distress.'

'Don't make fun of me, Jennifer. I was so embarrassed that I didn't know what to say. Yet, do you know, at the same time, deep down inside me, I was pleased that he had seen me. I

15

suppose I already wanted to be noticed by a good-looking mature man as a woman and not a kid.'

'Did he seize you in his arms and crush you to his breast, like in the movies?'

'Jennifer! Don't be silly. He pretended that he had not seen anything unusal but there was something about the way he looked at me that told me that he was interested in me.'

'Don't keep me in suspense. For heaven's sake, what happened?'

'I keep telling you, absolutely nothing. He asked me if I was lost and helped me get mounted.'

'Get mounted?'

'On my pony, you fool! Then, we rode home. That's all.'

'If that's all that happened, why do you remember it so vividly?'

'It was the way he held me as I got into the saddle. His hands sort of wandered. You know what I mean?'

'No. His hands could not wander very far if he were merely helping you up.'

Lucinda swallowed, then went on in a low voice.

'It was not quite like that. Somehow, when I saw him coming, I purposely took my time about pulling up my jeans. It was this strange feeling that I wanted to be seen. He was down off his horse in a flash and I felt his hands, fingering me. It was extraordinary. His hands were so big and rough but his touch was light and delicate. It was exciting: for the first time in my life, I felt that I was a woman. Then he bent over and kissed me.'

'You mean, a real genital kiss,' Jennifer breathed, quoting a phrase which she had picked up from a magazine.

'No, you insist in trying to make a great passionate affair out of nothing. He kissed me, very lightly, on the lips. I looked up into his eyes. They were grey and cool and yet they seemed to be hiding depths of passion and of sadness. Does that sound silly?'

'No, no, go on.'

16

'He gave me a smile. It was as if he knew what I had been up to and what was going on in my mind. Then, he said to me, quietly and in a vibrant, low voice, "You've grown up, Lucinda, into a very handsome young lady."'

'What did you say?' asked Jennifer.

'Nothing,' Lucinda replied. 'Somehow, words would not come. My mouth was dry and there was a lump in my throat. I just blushed. His hands rested on my shoulders and then he gently dropped them on to my breasts. They were the hands of a man who had lived. Firm, manly hands, strong and capable. Yet they were not at all rough and I felt my skin tingling when he touched me. My nipples were straining up: that was something which had never happened to me before. I felt so excited. I wanted something from him but I didn't know yet what it was. He let his hands fall on to my stomach and somehow, at that moment, I knew that I was a woman – a real woman although I knew that I had not yet grown up. It was a funny, mixed up feeling.

'Then he pulled me close to him. I can still remember his smell. He had a very masculine sort of smell, like old tweeds and pipe tobacco. Strong but not sour. I wanted him to cuddle me and to snuggle up in his arms.

'Instead, he let his hands slide down my body. I was stiff and tense and I could hardly breathe. Then, he touched me, very gently stroking me. I kept my legs open to him. It was as though I was hypnotised. I could not stir a muscle. I felt hot and damp, you now what I mean? I wanted him but I was afraid at the same time.'

'And then did he enter you? Penetrate you?' Jennifer's head was still full of her memories of the torrid romances she had read.

Both girls giggled nervously.

'No, I keep telling you. It was nothing really. Nothing at all. Then, he took his hand away, pulled up my jeans and, when I had fastened them, helped me into the saddle. We rode away, and neither of us said another word.'

'But you felt good?'

'Great. It was as though I could still feel the pressure of his hand and the rhythm of the horse got to me. I can't describe it: it was as though I was being massaged and part of me was going numb – but nice numb, you know, not like at the dentists. And my skin was tingling and pricking. I suddenly found that I was drenched and I was going all hot and cold. I've often dreamed of that ride and of being taken by a man like Colonel Fortescue – a man who has lived, not some little boy, hardly out of short trousers.'

'You've got a father complex,' Jennifer informed her friend.

'You must be joking! You've seen my father.'

'It doesn't have to be your actual father, simply an older man. Perhaps somebody you would like to be your father but you desire him as a lover. I've read all about it.'

As they trotted back, Lucinda thought about Jennifer's words. She could imagine Colonel Fortescue's gentle but masterful hands feeling her as though she was a precious jewel, but the face which unexpectedly arose before her eyes was that of Merton Maxwell, another older man and an ideal father. But, of that, she said not a word to Jennifer. It was a feeling, too intimate to be put into words.

When they got back to the house, they found Merton in high spirits. He had worked hard, and by way of mental relaxation, was enjoying himself in concocting an elaborate meal. Glorious aromas drifted up from the kitchen and the house echoed as the great man contentedly sang to himself at the top of his voice.

'Get a move on if you girls want to take a shower before dinner.' He called. 'Time, tide and good food wait for no man.'

'Come and take a shower with me,' Jennifer said to Lucinda.

'OK. I'll fetch my towel. We could start a business and call it Share-A-Shower,' Lucinda laughed.

The two girls slipped out of their clothes. Their bodies were damp from sweat and hot from their exercise in the sunshine. Jennifer stepped under the streaming, cold water and gave a little shiver of shock and of delight. As Lucinda went to join her, she looked admiringly at the lithe, graceful body of her friend.

Tiny droplets of water glistened on Jennifer's arms and legs like jewels. Her long hair clung to her head and shoulders as, with her eyes closed, she rubbed soap in a foamy white lather into the fragrant grottos between her legs and under her arms. Lucinda found herself experiencing a wave of desire for Jennifer's loveliness. Without knowing exactly why, she wanted to lick the beads of water off her beloved's firm, young breasts which glowed rosy pink, tiny buttons which only hinted at their future splendour.

'Come on, slow coach. What are you waiting for?' Jennifer shouted to Lucinda. 'Why are you standing and looking at me like that?'

Lucinda shook her head and murmured, with a touch of envy, 'I wish that I had a body like yours. So agile and strong but so slim and-oh, so sexy.'

Jennifer took her hand and pulled her close under the tumbling water.

'Don't be silly, Lucinda, darling. Your body is every bit as nice as mine. In fact, I think that it's better. I'm too skinny but you, well, you aren't exactly chubby, you're just right.'

She threw her arms around Lucinda and gave her a shower-soaked kiss on her cheek. Although the water was cold, Lucinda felt herself glowing and inside, she was radiantly hot. She squeezed Jennifer tight, thrilling to the tautness of her flawless skin against her own and feeling the exciting warmth of her body.

'Aren't you kids nearly ready?' Merton called.

'Coming,' his daughter shouted.

Jennifer turned up the heat of the shower and they rinsed the last of the soap from themselves before hurrying out to

19

towel themselves off.

'Do you really find me pretty?' Lucinda asked.

By way of answer, Jennifer kissed her upturned face again.

'You are not just pretty, Lucinda. Believe me, you are already a desirable young woman. We are not in school now, so stop thinking like a schoolgirl. Now, hurry up and get dressed or we shall both be in disgrace with the master of the house.'

Lucinda ran back into her own room and quickly put on a simple dress of emerald green. She glanced at her reflection in the mirror. The dress embraced her, fitting closely over the curves of her body and giving a suggestion of voluptuousness. Maybe there was some truth in what Jennifer had said. There was a femininity about her which Lucinda herself thought was appealing. She ran downstairs with a newly-found awareness of her own body giving a sparkle to her eyes and a jaunty spring to her step

As she went into the kitchen, Lucinda had a strange experience. She just knew that something extraordinary was going to happen. It was an impression which she could not explain. She sensed a thrill of anticipation as if she was embarking on some great adventure. As she was to say later, it was not a premonition for she felt no fear: it was simply as though there was an invisible presence in the house which was waiting for the moment to make itself felt and that moment was fast approaching.

'Is that you, Jenny?' Merton called from the kitchen.

'No, Jennifer is still upstairs, changing.'

'Well, I expect she'll be down in a minute. Do get yourself something to drink and be an angel and bring me a whisky please, Lucinda. I've got my hands full with the cooking. If I turn my back, everything will go up in flames.'

Lucinda went over to the cocktail cabinet. She was not sure how much whisky to put in the glass, so she decided to err on the side of generosity. She usually took a Coke or an orange juice, but tonight she felt very grown up and mixed herself a gin and tonic, the way she had seen it done at parties or on television. She carried the drinks into the kitchen. Merton, in his shirt-sleeves, was energetically stirring a saucepan, while other pots were bubbling encouragingly on the stove.

'Is there anything I can do to help?'

'No, thank you all the same, sweetheart. We great chefs are all individualists. Just pass me the cup that cheers. God, what a lot of whisky. I only want a drink, dear, not a bath. Or are you trying to get me tipsy?'

Merton took the whisky and added some ice and water.

'What have you got in your glass?' he asked. 'You're a bit young to hit the bottle, aren't you?'

'I just felt like something' Lucinda replied defensively.

'Good for you,' Merton laughed. Then his expression changed. 'I must stop treating you like a child, Lucinda. You are a woman – a real woman.'

Lucinda met his gaze. For the first time in her life, a man was looking at her as though she were a desirable, mature, young woman.

Jennifer walked into the kitchen and the tension between them vanished.

'Daddy, I feel awful. I think I caught a cold this afternoon.'

'Do you want to get to bed, Jenny? I'll bring your dinner upstairs on a tray?'

'No, that wouldn't be fair on Lucinda – nor on you. I'm not dying, you know. I think I'll take a leaf out of Lucinda's book and take a strong drink.'

'In you go. The food will be ready in a couple of minutes. Just lay the table for me, will you, my love.'

By the time that the two girls had set the table, Merton was bringing in the first course. It was a beautifully presented Coquille St Jacques and Merton poured a lightly chilled Chablis for them.

'This is all rather splendid,' Jennifer remarked, 'Are we celebrating something?'

Her father nodded. 'I've been going over the lines of this

new play. There comes a time when everything falls into place – that is, if the play is any good. Today, I suddenly knew that we have a winner. So, I feel happy and what better excuse do I need for feeding my delectable womenfolk?'

The dinner was a resounding success. Merton's sauce béarnaise was just right for the tournedos and he opened a choice bottle of Château Pape-Clément. After cheese and fruit, Lucinda felt relaxed and perhaps a trifle unsteady from the wine. But there was a contented, warm glow inside her. Jennifer, on the other hand, excused herself, saying that her head throbbed and she was running a slight temperature.

'Go up to bed then, poppet. There isn't a lot of clearing up to do.'

'I'll give you a hand, Merton,' Lucinda was glad to feel that she could be useful and Merton's grateful smile gave her pleasure.

The debris of the meal was soon removed, the dishwasher loaded and the decanters put away.

'I'm going to have a brandy: will you join me?' Merton picked up one of his big, balloon brandy glasses.

'No, I think I've had enough to drink.'

'Well, sit down and keep me company anyway.'

'I think that I ought to go up and see how Jennifer is.' Lucinda felt far too comfortable and it was so snug and cozy, she really did not feel like moving. As if he had read her thoughts, Merton shook his head and said.

'She'll have taken a couple of aspirins and should be sleeping by now. Leave her alone and don't disturb her.'

He settled down on the couch beside her and gently patted her arm. He took a sip of his brandy and then asked.

'Would you like some music?'

Lucinda nodded. 'Something dreamy.'

Merton thought for a moment and then selected a cassette which he put on his hi-fi stereo. The room was filled with the sound of soft, sweet strings. The music seemed to surround Lucinda and caress her: it was like luxuriating in a warm

22

bath. Merton slipped his arm around her shoulders.

'Happy?' he asked.

Lucinda nodded with a smile. Ever so tenderly, he drew her close to him and kissed her on the lips. It was so unexpected and yet, in some strange way, it seemed inevitable. Lucinda realized that, without being aware of it, she had been waiting for his lips to touch hers ever since they had met.

'You know, you are a very pretty girl, Lucinda.'

She did not know what to say or what she ought to do. Merton stroked her hair: she tingled at the touch of his fingers.

'Merton, it's not right. Think of Jennifer.' Lucinda's protest sounded feeble even to her own ears. His hand was on her shoulder and moving towards her breast. She made no attempt to push him away. Despite her words, her body wanted him.

'It's nothing to do with Jenny. This is just you and I, Lucinda. You were a child, now you are a woman. Dare to love, Lucinda, my lovely!'

As he spoke, Merton's hand had slipped the strap of her dress off her shoulder and it now cupped her milky white breast. He held her so gently and yet so firmly. The blood was throbbing in her veins and she found herself gasping for breath. Eagerly she turned up her face and sought his lips again, thrusting her tiny, pink tongue feverishly into the moistness of his mouth. Merton held her tight: their embrace seemed to stretch to eternity. Lucinda was faint with desire when Merton left her mouth and buried his face in her breast, licking and fondling her nipple, which stiffened as her passion mounted.

She got to her feet; the white dress fluttered to the ground and she stood before him, naked except for her gauzy, nylon panties which did little to conceal the fuzz of fine, golden hair. His eyes feasted on her beauty.

Her surrender was absolute and he caressed her like some precious gem. Without taking his eyes off her for an instant, he slowly undid his belt, unzipped his trousers and removed them. He completed undressing and turned the lights low. Then, reverently, lovingly, he laid Lucinda on the big, velvet sofa and lowered himself on to her impatient, burning body.

The sensation of a mature, male body was a totally new experience for her. Of course, she knew what to expect but she could not foretell what it would really be like. The taste of his lips, the aroma of his body, they were wonderfully different from anything she had known. She felt his firmness pressing against her own yielding flesh. The thick, curly hairs, like little jet black springs, on Merton's chest rubbing against her satiny smoothness set her skin tingling. Her hands explored, diffidently and wonderingly this new, masculine universe. He was powerful: she sensed it. There was a tension in his arms and legs and chunky body but it was a sort of inner force. Merton did not boast those exaggerated, thick knotted muscles such as Lucinda had seen in magazine advertisements, but Merton Maxwell possessed a strength that was far more convincing. He was gentle with her but with the gentleness of the truly strong, like a potter moulding a delicate vessel, loving, tender, yet firm.

Lucinda longed for and dreaded the moment. But first, Merton's hands and mouth possessed her and everything seemed to unfold like a dream. She felt no pain, only long, languorous ecstasy. Their bodies were one, as though they had been made for each other. Her satisfaction was complete. Lucinda had learned to love and she knew that for the rest of her life, she would never be content with anything less than total, passionate commitment. Surely it would never be the same with anybody else; only Merton could give her that degree of exquisite pleasure.

Strange she thought, that after such a wild racing of the blood, such burning intensity, there should be such a sense of utter peace, so complete a feeling of fulfilment. Time ceased to exist. She and Merton were the only people in the world and the miracle of that moment would never, never come to an end.

They lay in each other's arms for a long time. Then Merton climbed to his feet and picked Lucinda up.

'It's very late, my sweet. Time for bed.'

He carried her across the room and up the stairs to her own bed. She had her arms around his neck, sleepily savouring his rich, musky scent. Her body glowed until it was soothed by the cool embrace of her sheets.

'Goodnight, my lover,' she whispered.

'Sleep well, Lucinda, my lovely,' Merton answered, as he brushed his lips against hers and then tiptoed out of her room.

Next morning, Jennifer's cold had disappeared and she was her usual, sprightly self again. Merton, on the other hand, seemed strangely reserved, as if he feared that in the cold light of the morning Lucinda might regret the adventure of that memorable night; Lucinda wanted to reassure him, but was afraid of speaking in front of Jennifer.

The two girls were walking in the sheltered rose garden at the back of the house when Jennifer, without any warning, stared earnestly at Lucinda and demanded, 'Have you and my father become lovers?'

Lucinda was so startled that she could not reply. She felt her cheeks blushing crimson. Jennifer laughed.

'It's all right. You don't have to explain or apologize. I've got used to reading the signs. He goes all quiet as if he is ashamed of what he's done. And you are all starry-eyed and walking on air. When he comes into the room, you break out in a hot flush.'

Lucinda forced herself to laugh.

'Come on, Jennifer! You've been reading too many romantic novels!'

'Lucinda, I really don't mind. Daddy just has something that attracts women and he needs their love. Perhaps it's because he's a great artist. I don't know, but without the adoration of beautiful women he would shrivel up. It's the food which keeps him alive. That's why Mummy left him: she simply could not stand it. But with me, it's different. I

25

understand what that means to him. And he's fond of you, Lucinda. I know, I've watched him. Be kind to him. I swear that if you hurt him, I shall never forgive you.'

With a sob, Lucinda threw herself into Jennifer's arms. They hugged each other and then Jennifer pushed Lucinda gently away.

'Why don't you go inside to him, now?'

Lucinda ran into the house. Merton was in his study. She burst in and, without a word, threw herself into his arms. He clasped her to him and kissed her.

'Jenny's been talking to you?'

Lucinda nodded.

'God, how that girl knows me. She reads my soul like an open book. If you love me, Lucinda, I want you to love her too. We are so close that everything we have is shared. I adore you and I have loved many women before you but Jennifer is the one person in my life. You probably can't understand that but it's the two of us against the world.'

'No, Merton, don't say that. I want to be part of your life – yours and Jennifer's. Don't shut me out!'

'Dear, sweet, Lucinda! No, we could never exclude you.'

They went out into the garden. Jennifer saw them coming towards her, arm in arm, her father and her best friend. She was wonderfully happy.

The rest of the holiday passed all too quickly. The three of them were so completely in harmony that there was never a cross word. Lucinda was never again to experience such complete bliss: no love is ever quite as intense as the first love. Now that there was no need for pretence, she moved into Merton's room and they made love gently, tenderly but with an inner fire which consumed them.

'I don't know how I shall ever be able to put up with life at home again,' Lucinda complained as the time for her departure approached.

'Oh, come now, my lovely, it won't be as bad as that.' Merton accepted their parting as if it were the end of the run of one of his plays, something to look back on with nostalgia.

'Merton, you are heartless. You just don't care.'

'Now, Lucinda, that's not true. But I know that we shall meet again and that our love will last. You have to go home to your parents, so it's no use making a great melodrama of it. And I know something else. Since you came to me here, you have developed a capacity for feeling that you will keep always. I shall not be the only man in your life, Lucinda, whatever you may think now. You are so emotional and you have such depths of passion that you must love just as you must breathe. No one person will be sufficient for all your affection. Mark my words, for I know you better than you know yourself.'

As time went by, Lucinda was to remember what Merton had said and to admit to herself that he was right.

2

It was late afternoon when Merton drove Lucinda up to the front door of the dignified house in Belgrave Square. Her father was not at home, but her brother, Miles, greeted Merton with rather more formality than was natural in someone who was still a few months short of his twentieth birthday.

'It was awfully kind of you to put up with my kid sister for so long, Mr Maxwell. I do hope that she has behaved and not been a dreadful nuisance.'

'On the contrary, Lucinda has been splendid company, both for my daughter and for myself. She will always be welcome whenever she feels like paying us a visit.'

That's put Miles in his place, Lucinda thought happily. Serves him right for being such a frightful snob. Merton had a TV session the next day and he had decided to spend the night at his Hampstead flat. Jennifer had been left behind to look after the 'cottage' and she had kissed Lucinda goodbye so tenderly that nobody would have thought that the two girls would be reunited in only about three weeks time at Hurstmonbury. Miles had got back that day from a holiday in Italy and he and Lucinda were to spend the night in their London home before going, next day, to the family's country house in Devon.

Merton only stayed a few minutes before taking his leave. His farewells to Lucinda were cordial but very correct. Miles could never have guessed that they were lovers. I suppose that is one advantage of having an affair with an actor, Lucinda thought with an innner chuckle. She did not look forward to being questioned by her brother about her holiday but she need not have worried. Miles was full of stories of his own vacation. He had falled in love also, but not with any woman. He had left his heart in Florence and he insisted in treating his sister to a verbal tour of the Uffizi and the Pitti Galleries. That took them until dinner and after the meal, he launched out on an account of the splendours of Siena. Lucinda half heard his words: she was still reliving the last embrace of Merton, the pressure of his hand still weighed on her breasts, her thighs were still moist with the sensation of his nearness. She excused herself shortly after dinner and went to her room, saying that she was tired from the journey and wanted to get a good night's rest before the long day's travelling that was ahead of them in the morning.

The train journey to Devon was long and uneventful. Lucinda passed the time, reading a light, romantic novel, much to the annoyance of her serious-minded brother.

'Really, Lucinda, what do you want to read that tripe for? Love stories,' Miles sneered. 'What does a kid of your age know about love?'

His sister said nothing, but her eyes were dancing.

Their father's chauffeur-driven car was waiting for them at the station and took them swiftly home. In fact, home for Lucinda was a magnificent mansion, very like the great country house which she had seen on the way to Merton's 'cottage'.

Miles and Lucinda were the only children of Gerald Farrer, fifteenth Viscount Hamblewood.

The estate in Devon had been in the possession of the family since the seventeenth century, when Matthew Farrer had bravely and loyally fought for his king against the Parliamentarians and had been ennobled by the grateful Charles II at the Restoration. The Merry Monarch had made dukes of the bastard sons of his mistresses and mere viscounts of his soldiers and statesmen who had supported his cause, but the Hamblewoods prospered and the fourth viscount built the great house which was Lucinda's home. But the more recent Farrers had not gone into either trade or industry and the family fortunes had gradually faded. Lucinda's father, a tall, balding and rather shy gentleman of no great distinction, had retrieved the situation with a well calculated marriage. His wife, Melanie, was the heiress of a Connecticut family which had shown the same single-minded devotion in the pursuit of wealth that the first Viscount Hamblewood had in the service of his king. Melanie's great grandfather, being a man without embarassing principles, had sold arms to both sides in the Civil War and made a fortune. He had thus established one of America's leading banking families. Melanie's marriage to Gerald brought the distinction of the English aristocracy to the upstart Yankee, while she brought to him the money that he needed for the upkeep of the Devon estate which bore his name, and the house in Belgrave Square, which was Melanie's family's wedding gift.

Both Miles and Lucinda had taken for granted the possession of wealth and a privileged place in society from the day that each of them had been born. Both children had been sent to expensive boarding schools and, at Hurstmonbury, Lucinda had mixed exclusively with the children of other rich or noble families. Lucinda was not a snob. It was simply that she had never been in contact with the lives of poor or working people. The Maxwells were hardly proletarians, yet they were probably the nearest thing to what passes as ordinary folk in English society that Lucinda had ever known.

Of course, there were the servants, both at Hamblewood and in London, but Melanie, the girl from democratic USA, far more than her upper class English husband, maintained the strictest of class distinctions and allowed no familiarity with her children on the part of mere maids and menservants.

So Lucinda's childhood was sheltered and now, after her taste of freedom with Jennifer and Merton, she was, for the first time, aware of just how restricted her life was at home. Yet, although her romance with Merton was the first time that she had been truly in love and savoured the joys of sex, there had been an episode in her life which gave her a mild foretaste of the emotional upheavals which life had in store for her.

Some two years ago, George had been head gardener at Hamblewood. Lucinda had laid her hands on a smuggled copy of *Lady Chatterley's Lover* which she read in awe and amazement. Could it be that men and women behaved like that, glorying in their sexuality? And could it be that a well bred, respectable milady, like her mother, could indulge her wild passion with a mere servant? Lucinda looked around at the domestic staff at Hamblewood with a new interest. And her eyes fell on George. He was a well built man in his mid-thirties. It was a pity that he was not a gamekeeper, but surely a head gardener would be an acceptable substitute? However, Viscountess Hamblewood showed no passionate attraction towards George. Indeed, she seemed to be oblivious of his existence.

Lucinda considered her mother's apparent indifference and, absolutely certain in her identification of Melanie with Lawrence's heroine, decided that the lovers must be concealing their affair. She was consumed with curiosity and pursued George relentlessly. All her spare time, she wandered around the grounds of Hamblewood, never far from where

George would be working. She never came across Melanie, but she did meet Tim.

Tim was a fair-haired, freckle-faced, snub-nosed fifteen year old. During the school holidays, Tim came to Hamblewood with George, his father, and Lucinda saw him a couple of times in the grounds of the house before she first spoke to him.

It was a hot, lazy day. Lucinda was wearing a flimsy, white blouse and skimpy shorts, but her skin glowed with the kiss of the sun. Just the weather, she reflected, to bring the hidden lust of Lady Chatterley–Melanie for her gamekeeper–gardener lover to boiling point. The young girl crossed the wide lawn and picked her way into the shrub-surrounded, flower gardens. After a short while, she spotted George. He was staking dahlias which were growing in a well-tended bed. There was no sign of her mother but, walking away from George, there was that pleasant looking boy again. He smiled at her.

'Hello,' Lucinda said, 'who are you?'

'My name's Tim. That's my Dad.' The boy pointed to George.

The two youngsters walked together: George took no notice of them. At the end of the gardens was a large, ornamental lake and this was Lucinda's favourite spot. She would lie by the water edge, hidden from view by tall reeds which fringed the lake. She led Tim there and the two of them squatted beside the lake. They watched a trio of ducks, swimming past in strict formation: a honey laden bee bumbled around their noses. The world was at peace.

'Have you seen my mother?' Lucinda asked.

Tim shook his head.

'I think that she is in love with your father,' Lucinda said boldly. 'Do you think that George loves her?'

Tim was wide-eyed with astonishment.

'No, of course not. My Dad loves my Mum. And anyway, your mother isn't all that pretty. Not like you are.'

'Do you find me pretty?' Lucinda was intrigued by this unexpected turn of their conversation.

The boy flushed and turned his head away.

'Go on. Tell me!' Lucinda urged.

Tim swallowed and, in a subdued voice, muttered, 'Yes. I think that you are very pretty.' He raised his eyes and dared to meet her gaze. 'I would like to kiss you.'

Lucinda considered this proposition. She found him a good looking boy and she had never before received a tribute from a male admirer. Maybe she would turn out to be the incarnation of Lady Chatterley herself instead of Melanie.

'Well, go on then. Kiss me.'

The boy approached her shyly. He held her awkwardly and very self-consciously placed his mouth against hers. She felt the pressure of his lips and he began to pull away.

'No, not like that, silly,' Lucinda had seen enough films to know that there was a lot more to kissing than that.

She pulled him towards her and put her arms around his neck. Her tongue pushed into Tim's mouth and suddenly she felt him respond. He gripped her and his embrace took her breath away.

'That's enough' she panted.

But Tim did not release her. Rather, he hugged her more tightly and his lips sought hers feverishly. She could feel the heat of his body through his T-shirt and the salty smell of his sweat was in her nostrils.

'Let me touch you there,' the boy pleaded.

Fascinated, Lucinda felt his hands grope up the legs of her shorts. His skin was smooth yet firm and her excitement rose as he caressed her, tentatively. His fingers were gentle as though she were some precious, fragile object and he was afraid of hurting or damaging her.

'Do you like that?' she breathed.

Tim nodded.

It felt good, but he was not sure of what was needed, Lucinda took his hand and guided it, so that the play of his fingers was in the right place.

'You are wet,' Tim's voice was hoarse.

'That's good. Just stroke me like you are doing.'

She withdrew her own hand, undid the boy's trousers and pulled down his underpants. It was the first time that the young girl had ever seen a male sex organ. Of course, she had read books and seen pictures but somehow, literally in the flesh, it was still different. She did not know rightly what she had expected. Tim's penis was quite long but very slender. It looked as though it was staring at her through the hood of its foreskin. Lucinda decided that it was not pretty, yet it fascinated her. It was begging to be touched. She took his bulging erection in the palm of her hand. She could feel the throbbing of the blood through his veins. It was satin smooth to her touch and she rubbed the tense, straining penis softly.

'Harder! Please, do it harder.'

She obeyed. Tim gasped. His muscles went rigid and his hands seized her convulsively. His eyes were glazed and he was gulping as though he could not get enough air. It was nice what Tim was doing to her but she was amazed at the effect her nimble fingers were having on the boy. He writhed and wriggled as if he were in agony but his flushed cheeks and faint, choked cries betrayed his ecstasy. Lucinda had a sudden insight of her power over him. To every subtle change of pressure or speed in her relentless massage, Tim responded immediately. Her fingers commanded and he obeyed, blindly, slavishly. The thought flashed through Lucinda's mind that if she went on doing it faster and faster, she could drive him mad. As he grew more and more subservient to her masterful hands, Tim's own hands dropped nervelessly to his side and she took over entirely. She felt good. It was not the way she had read about it in *Lady Chatterley's Lover*, but there was something very satisfying in having the boy so completely under her control and in driving him into a frenzy.

'Please, don't stop. Please, faster. Oh, yes, yes, please.'

His voice was a mere whimper. His eyes were tight shut and

little beads of sweat stood out on his forehead. His twisting and turning became more and more convulsive. He was gripping her quite tight. It hurt but she did not mind, she was too intent on the crescendo of the boy's excitement until he suddenly gave a little scream and Lucinda felt the pulsing in her hand. She jerked it away.'

'Look, you've made me all wet.'

For some seconds, Tim could not speak. When he had recovered somewhat, he was all apologies and seemed ashamed of what he had done.

'Don't worry', Lucinda told him. 'It doesn't matter. Lend me your handkerchief.'

She rinsed her hand in the lake and then wiped it dry on Tim's handkerchief. Meanwhile, he had done up his trousers. Lucinda straightened her own clothes.

'I must be getting back before Mummy misses me.'

'May I see you again? Or are you too annoyed with me?'

All Tim's earlier shyness had returned but Lucinda patted his arm, as if to reassure him.

'I don't see why not, but we must be careful. I am sure that our parents would not be pleased if they knew.'

They strolled back. George gave his son an enquiring glance but said nothing.

During the next few weeks, Lucinda and Tim met several times, usually at the same place. During their spells of kissing, cuddling and immature lovemaking they were never disturbed and they never saw anybody.

But someone must have seen them. One morning, Tim was not there. Neither could Lucinda find George. She wandered about the grounds disconsolately and eventually she asked Miles what had become of the gardener. Her brother told her that he had gone to work for somebody else. From that day, she never saw George or Tim again.

3

'Lucie, I want to have a good talk with you.'

'Very well, Miles. But I do wish that you would stop calling me Lucie. You know I hate the name.'

They had finished their breakfast and Lucinda's parents had gone off, leaving their two children together in the dining-room.

'Come into the library.'

With a sigh, Lucinda followed her brother. She could not help comparing steady, stodgy Miles with Merton, so urbane, so witty, such good fun to be with and, oh God, such a good lover.

Miles settled in a deep armchair and favoured Lucinda with a superior, big-brother smile. He motioned to her to sit down.

'If you want to give me a further account of the art treasures of Italy, I think I have heard all that I can stand,' Lucinda complained.

'I want to talk about you.'

Lucinda's first reaction was one of panic. He must have found out about Merton. But how? Nobody has said anything and when they were frolicking happily in bed, Miles was hundreds of miles away. Miles away, but now Miles is here: she played with the words while she awaited an outburst from her brother.

'I spoke to Father this morning, before you were out of bed, Lucinda.'

'About me?'

'About you.'

How like Miles to go behind my back and talk to Daddy before I had a chance to say anything, Lucinda's mind raced. But, what could I have said, what sort of explanation would make sense to the fifteenth Viscount Hamblewood?

Damn them all, they would not be able to take Merton away from her. Her brain was on fire. She had found the love of her life and mother, father, brother would never divide them. She was ready to fight the whole family rather than be forced to renounce the man who had opened for her the doorway to life and love.

Lucinda glared at her brother like a tigress, ready to fight for the life of its threatened mate.

'You're no longer a child and it's time that you made some plans for the future,' Miles intoned.

Lucinda stared at him, in uncomprehending silence. Was it possible that he was so old-fashioned that he was going to insist on matrimony after her very first mature, sexual encounter? That was going a bit far, these days, even for someone as prim and proper as Miles.

'Times have changed and we cannot live in the past.'

Good God, he really ought to be a clergyman, thought Lucinda. He could not even ask the time without delivering a sermon. But now what is he getting at?

'Look at me, for example.'

Lucinda shuddered at the unappetizing prospect.

'One day, I shall be the sixteenth Viscount.' Miles was at his most pompous and Lucinda felt an urge to punch him on the nose. 'But, shall we still have all this?'

Miles waved his hand to indicate all the signs of splendour and wealth which surrounded them. 'Mark my words, my sister, the days of the idle rich are passing away. Just because our father is rich, we should not get any false ideas of what is in store for us. Neither you nor I have any excuse for not being able to earn our own livings.'

'Mother is the rich one,' Lucinda corrected quietly.

'Don't quibble!' Miles was offended.

Lucinda could not see what all this had to do with her affair with Merton, but she could not resist teasing Miles.

'I was just pointing out that if you do not feel inclined to work for a living, you could follow our glorious family tradition and marry a rich heiress,' she pointed out with a great display of good humour.

'That is no way to talk about our parents,' retorted the furious Miles. 'You know that not a cross word has ever passed between them and they have led a blameless married life. You ought to have more respect for them and try to behave as if you were proud of being a Farrer.'

Jolly good, exulted Lucinda. That's got him going and, with any luck, off the subject of Merton. But what was her brother talking about? Perhaps he was leading up to something else.

'I do not intend to marry for money,' Miles snapped. 'What I am telling you is that we have to be able to work and that means being properly qualified. That's why I am studying Law. I'll get my degree at Oxford and then I'll be able to get a job with one of the big firms in the City or in some multinational. That's where the future lies. The world does not owe me a living simply because one of my ancestors did rather well three hundred years ago. And what I am trying to get into your head, my dear, scatter-brained sister, is that the same goes for you too. One day, you'll have to leave Hamblewood and find your own place in the world. And what will you be able to do?'

'Oh, is that all you wanted to talk about?' Lucinda laughed in relief, much to the annoyance of her brother.

'You are impossible, Lucinda. Can't you be serious for a few minutes?'

How typical of her parents, Lucinda thought, to leave it to Miles to discuss her future with her. Her mother was probably off somewhere, opening a bazaar or graciously receiving a bishop, while her father might be planning the next expedition to a Scottish grouse moor or a descent on a trout stream. But Miles was sober, Miles was serious. He would be responsible for himself and for his young sister. But he would be middle aged by the age of twenty.

Miles was droning on. He was explaining to Lucinda that if she wanted to avoid starving to death at some vague date in the future, she had better decide now how to conclude her education with a career in mind.

The trouble was that Lucinda had no idea of what she wanted to do when she left school. She could dream of a stage career, playing opposite Merton's Romeo perhaps, but she had to admit to herself that she had to acting talent.

'You are not a great intellect.' Miles pronounced judgement with an arrogant self-assurance. 'However, you will probably be quite decent looking when you've lost the puppy fat: you might get a job as a model or something else that's not too demanding.'

'How dare you, Miles, you pompous prig!' Lucinda flared up. 'I am just as capable as you are of earning my living in some stupid office. I'll get a job – a better job than you. Or maybe, I'll become an author. I've thought about writing for a long time.'

'I'm delighted to hear that you have given the matter some thought. Although I don't see you as another Jan Austen.'

'I could be a second Xaviera Hollander—' Lucinda retorted.

'Who?' asked Miles.

'Oh, never mind. You wouldn't understand her books, Miles.'

'Well, just you think about what I have said.' Miles felt that he had made his point and he made a dignified exit.

Although Lucinda heartily loathed Miles, she knew that the time had come for her to think seriously of her future. Whatever happened, she would do what she wanted and not what Miles or anybody else told her to do.

4

Lucinda looked into the eyes of Michael Johnson and decided that she liked what she saw. He shifted uncomfortably under her gaze and nervously shuffled the papers which were strewn on his desk.

'Now, let me see, Miss Farrer, when I can next find time for you.'

I wouldn't mind finding plenty of time for you, Lucinda thought. He can't be more than three or four years older than I am and he has gorgeous, soft eyes. I wonder what he looks like undressed. I hope he has a hairy chest: I love men with a thick forest of hair on their bodies.

Michael Johnson interrupted her reverie.

'I really don't have much time during the day. Would you find it too inconvenient to come to my rooms again next Tuesday. Let's say at nine?'

'No, that will be prefectly all right.'

He really is very shy. He is blushing and he is frightened to look me in the eyes. Lucinda was amused by the confusion which she caused in her tutor. I bet he has never had a woman in his life.

'See you next Tuesday, then, Miss Farrer.'

'The name is Lucinda, Mr Johnson.'

'Oh yes. Of course, Lucinda.'

He had a North Country burr to his voice which Lucinda found unfamiliar and attractive. She bestowed a dazzling smile on the embarrassed young man, picked up her notebook and, pulling her black undergraduate gown around her shoulders walked out of his study.

Two years had elapsed since that conversation with Miles in the library at Hamblewood and Lucinda was still no more decided on her future career. The idea of writing had persisted and so she had agreed when it had been suggested at school that she should read English Literature at university.

'You are quite a bright, young thing,' her headmistress had commented. 'I don't see why you should not try for a place at Oxford.'

'My brother is at Oxford,' Lucinda replied.

'Well, that's nice. He will be company for you.'

'Thank you very much,' Lucinda said, 'but I think that I would prefer Cambridge.'

That is how the Honourable Lucinda Farrer came to be leaving the rooms of her tutor, Michael Johnson, on her way back to her own room in the Great Court of Trinity College. There were a handful of girls from Hurstmonbury up at Cambridge but none of them were among Lucinda's close friends. Jennifer had left school the year before and had gone out to California where Merton was making a series of films. Lucinda had seen him a couple of times before he left, but they had never had the opportunity to repeat that idyllic holiday in his 'cottage'. Lucinda had written to him, but Merton was a poor correspondent and many months had passed since she had last heard from him. There had been other boy friends but none of them lasted more than a few weeks.

As Miles had forecast, Lucinda had matured into a very attractive young woman. Heads turned when she passed and she was aware of the effect that she had on men, and she was sufficiently vain and mischievous to blast some unfortunates with the full force of her charm. Like Michael Johnson.

Lucinda was settling down easily enough in her first term. She had been lucky in getting rooms in the college so that she had only a few minutes walk to lectures and tutorials while the best of the restaurants, cafes and shops were clustered just outside the walls of the college. She was besieged by enthusiastic students urging her to join every conceivable society, political, religious, social, sporting and downright eccentric. For centuries, Trinity, like the other old colleges, had been exclusively male and even now, women were very much in the minority both in the college and in the university as a whole. Consequently, a pretty girl was much in demand. Lucinda avoided getting too closely involved until she got herself and her work organized. And her work meant Michael Johnson.

On her arrival at Trinity, Lucinda had been summoned to two interviews. The first was a rather elderly and very senior member of the college who informed her that he was her Moral Tutor.

'I am not concerned with your work,' Dr Parkinson informed her drily. 'However, somebody has to be responsible for each junior member of the college and it has fallen to me to watch over you. If you have any problems of a private nature – personal or domestic, I'm the chap you come to. Understood? If you want permission to go home for your grandmother's wedding or your pet budgerigar breaks its leg, you will find me sympathetic and helpful. To be serious, many young men and women get themselves emotionally tied up in knots or find the work too great a strain. My door is always open to you.'

Lucinda thanked Dr Parkinson and devoutly hoped that she would not be obliged to see too much of him. Despite his easy manner and his words, she had the impression that her Moral Tutor might prove to be a tough-minded man and not at all in harmony with the permissive society which everybody talked about. With any luck, she might get away with one invitation to tea each term and some polite but uninterested conversation about her home and family.

Her other interview was with another senior Fellow of the college. Mr Snell was the author of a number of books of literary criticism and was a scholar whose work was already known to Lucinda. He had made a highly successful television series and was something of a national celebrity. He explained that he was her Director of Studies and went over the curriculum with her, advising her which lectures she should attend and allocating her to other tutors for work on individual subjects.

'You had better go to Miss Cavendish for Elizabethan Drama: she's out at Girton. Call her up and make an appointment. The most practical way to get out there is by bike. As for The English Novel, I've put you down to go to Mr Johnson. He's in college. You'll find his rooms in the second court – Neville's Court it's called – on the other side of the hall. I had a word with him just before you came in and fixed a time for you. Drop in on him next Tuesday evening, about quarter past eight. It's a bit late, but he is pretty well booked up at the beginning of term. By the way, young Johnson is also giving a course of lectures on Women Novelists, he's particularly good on George Eliot and Mrs Gaskell. You could do worse than go and hear what he has to say.'

And that was how Lucinda came to meet Michael Johnson.

The day before her appointment for her first tutorial with him, she went to the opening lecture of the series given by Michael Johnson. The hall was crowded: several hundred young men and women were following the advice of their directors of studies and giving 'young Johnson' a try. Lucinda found herself among a group of about a dozen girls who were chattering to themselves before the arrival of the lecturer. A couple of them were avowed feminists, intent on making sure that no unfortunate lady novelist suffered violence at the hands of a pretentious male intellectual.

The appearance of Michael Johnson excited some comment and even murmurs of approval from some of the female students. He was quite tall but he hunched his shoulders slightly as if he did not want to draw attention to himself. Everything about Michael Johnson suggested shyness. His dark brown eyes darted nervous glances at the assembled throng. He rubbed his chin pensively and then fiddled with a pair of horn-rimmed spectacles which, however, he never put on once during the whole hour of the lecture. He was possibly thirty but he had a sort of childlike vulnerability which appealed to the more maternally minded of his audience.

'Now that's a guy I could really dig,' commented Lucinda's neighbour, a burly Amazon from Los Angeles.

A stately Indian girl, in a richly embroidered silk sari, nodded agreement.

The lecturer stood silently before them while he arranged and rearranged a sheaf of notes and reference books.

'I wonder whether he screws,' remarked the non-angelic lady from Los Angeles.

'I wouldn't mind finding out,' said a pretty English undergraduate, siting on the other side of Lucinda.

'Honey, that sort of man needs leading all the way.' The American girl spoke as if she had a wealth of experience to draw on. 'You wouldn't even get to first base. No, I've made up my mind to take the poor goof in hand. He may be the lecturer, but I'll look after his education. Just you watch, I'll have him in bed before half term.'

She flashed a smile of triumph around her, as if the feat had already been achieved.

Lucinda felt as if she had been thrown into the middle of a female jury, busy passing their verdict on the presentability of their intended victim. A surge of annoyance passed through her, as she listened to the comments of the pack of would-be man-eaters. In particular, she resented the self confidence of the young American student. Who the hell did she think she was and why was she so special that no man could resist her ample charms?

Lucinda felt an immediate sympathy for the man who had begun to speak, quietly and unassumingly. He seemed pleasant and likeable and deserved somebody better than the bold Californian big game hunter who was watching him with a knowing smile as she licked her lips. The Indian girl had said nothing, but the intent look in her eyes spoke louder than words. Surely, Michael Johnson was doomed: if he did not fall to one of the birds of prey, then he must be snatched up by another. But such a nice young man was worth somebody better than any of these girls sitting around her. Somebody like her, perhaps?

Why not? She could not help thinking how amusing it would be if she were to carry off the prize. And it would save Michael from the proverbial fate worse than death.

Some of the girls even listened to the lecture and took notes. Despite his reticence, Michael spoke fluently and he held his audience by his obvious sincerity and sound scholarship. He put his subject over without any false flamboyance or empty

43

oratory. When he finished, there was a buzz of approval, as the students gathered up their notebooks and started to file out of the hall.

'Before you go, Mr Johnson, please, can I ask you a question?' The American girl was opening her attack and she galloped down the stairs of the tiered room to put some point to the young man who was cornered behind the lectern.

Lucinda bit her lip and felt more resolved than ever to intervene, if it were at all possible, for the good of Michael Johnson's body, if not his soul.

The following day, Lucinda dined, along with some hundreds of fellow students, in the centuries-old dining hall. The food was mediocre, but the setting magnificent. Afterwards, back in her rooms, she prepared to descend upon her tutor. She picked up her notebook and slipped on her gown. She was on the point of leaving when, as an afterthought, she sprayed herself liberally with her favourite perfume, an exotic and sensuous scent, which always did something for her when she wore it.

It was in a confident mood that she left her rooms and strode across the broad expanse of Great Court through the 'Screens', the passage through the Hall, into the serene splendour of Neville's Court. In the far corner of the Court, tucked in to the angle where Wren's library separated Trinity from the peaceful waters of the tiny River Cam, was the staircase on which stood Michael Johnson's set of rooms. His heavy, oak, outer door stood open, indicating that he was in and could be disturbed. Lucinda tapped on the inner door and went in.

Michael Johnson was wearing the scruffiest, polo-necked wool pullover that Lucinda had ever seen and the young man's informal uniform was completed by a pair of stained, canary yellow, corduroy trousers and carpet slippers. He was busy, ramming tobacco into a wide bowled, cherry wood pipe, presumably with a view to making a few more holes in his tattered sweater.

'Make yourself at home. Take a seat and do get rid of that ridiculous gown.' He pointed to an armchair and Lucinda, feeling rather over-dressed for the occasion, complied.

For the next hour, Michael discussed her work with her and gave her an extensive reading list. He was a serious, earnest scholar but completely free from academic dryness. At the end of her tutorial, Lucinda prepared to depart, having been set an essay to write for the following week.

'Do you think you will be able to get through that amount of work before your next tutorial, Miss Farrer?'

She was determined to break through the armour of his formality.

'The name is Lucinda, Remember?'

'Yes, of course. Forgive me, Lucinda.'

A broad smile spread across his face. He's not bad, in fact, quite dishy when he stops playing the young professor, she thought. On an impulse, she turned towards him and asked, 'Where do you come from, Mr Johnson? You don't seem to be like the other lecturers here who ought to be stuffed and put in the museum.'

'That hardly shows the respect due to your elders,' he grinned. 'As a matter of fact, I'm from Bradford – a working-class lad from one of those solid, working-class towns. And, since you are Lucinda to me, my name is Michael.'

'Michael', she assented. 'I've never been to Bradford: you must tell me all about it.'

'Another time,' Michael replied, leading her to the door. 'Don't think me rude, but I have a lot of work to get through before the morning.'

Lucinda was not displeased with the evening. These things take time, she told herself, and I have made definite progress. Let's see how I get on, next week.

As it happened, she did not have to wait so long.

Lucinda had to buy a number of recommended text books and on the following Thursday afternoon she spent some time in the lavishly stocked bookshop across the road from Trinity. She staggered out of the doorway, peeping over the top of an immense armful of books, bumped straight into a passer-by and decanted learned tomes all over the pavement. The man with whom she had collided grabbed her elbow to prevent her from stumbling. Lucinda swore venomously and found herself looking up into the face of her tutor.

'Lucinda! Here, let me help you.'

Michael was on his knees, picking up her books and apologizing profusely. Together, they crossed the narrow street, adroitly dodging cars and bicycles and passed beneath the imposing gateway of Trinity. Lucinda was turning on to the path which led to her staircase, when Michael said, in a hesitant voice, 'Why don't you dump those books in your room and then come and have tea with me?'

Lucinda cast a mocking glance at him.

'Surely you don't have time? After all, you give me tutorials in the evening because your days are so full.'

'Even junior fellows of a college are allowed time off for tea.' His tone was partly humourous, but also defensive. 'I am going to have tea in my room and I would very much appreciate your company.'

His formality brought a smile to Lucinda's lips.

'I find your invitation irresistible.'

Up in Michael's rooms, he bustled about, putting a kettle on the gas ring, and producing from a cupboard, biscuits and a cake which he cut and placed on a plate.

'Afternoon tea at Cambridge is an ancient ritual. How do you like your tea?'

'Lemon and one spoon of sugar, please. I suppose all this is very different from life in Bradford?'

Michael laughed. 'Sure. There you would be expected to take milk in your tea. Lemon, indeed, you strange, foreign Southerners!'

'Foreigner?'

'Anybody born south of Manchester is a foreigner. Didn't you know?'

Michael chatted fluently, but Lucinda sensed an inner nervousness, as if all his sophistication were just a mask.

She got to her feet and, very deliberately, walked over to Michael. Her eyes were upon him and he stood as if hypnotized. Without a word, Lucinda pressed her lips on his and kissed him.

'Don't be scared, Michael. It's one of our foreign customs.'

Michael felt that she was mocking him and, at the same time, daring him. He had never met any woman like her. She was so young and yet so self-possessed – and so lovely. He put his hands on her elbows and drew her to him. His mouth thirsted for hers, she was as sweet as honey.

A wave of triumph surged through Lucinda. This man will be mine. The words pulsed in her brain. She could sense his growing excitement. Her soft, nimble fingers found his swelling, feverish penis.

'We'll have to do something about this,' she murmured, as she stroked and caressed him. Michael stumbled towards the bedroom, guiding her towards the bed. He was frightened that she would find him clumsy, but Lucinda seemed to know exactly how to respond to his passion. He stopped to lock the door and found that, in a flash, Lucinda had slipped out of her jeans and her blouse. She stood before him in the flimsiest of bra and panties: he had never in his life seen anybody so provocative, so alluring. Frenziedly, he ripped off his own clothes and went to lay Lucinda on the bed, but she avoided his grasp and pushed him on to the bed. Before he knew what was happening to him, she had dropped to her knees before him and taken him in her mouth.

The ecstasy was almost unbearable. He twisted and turned, writhing in pleasure and in torment. Her lips and her tongue possessed him. Every fibre of his being ached for

47

her but she was subduing him, enslaving him. Michael Johnson learnt what it meant to be seduced.

He wanted to hold back. He wanted to take her and to plunge his aching penis into her, to penetrate her so deeply that he could lose himself in her moist, soft sweetness. But it was as if his legs had turned to jelly and he could not pull himself away from the embrace of those lips which were so completely in command. His muscles were getting rigid, the veins were swelling in his cock. Lucinda could feel that he was near to climax. She clasped his thighs more tightly and she licked and sucked faster and faster. He was groaning and sobbing, his fingers in her hair, twitching spasmodically. She stripped him of the last vestiges of control and, with a cry of relief, he came and surrendered his thick, white sperm which she swallowed hungrily.

Michael collapsed on the bed. Lucinda calmly got up and went into his bathroom. He was still recovering when she walked back and quickly dressed.

'Next time, you will have to do that to me,' she told him. 'See you on Tuesday, tutor mine!'

She walked to the door and as she left, turned to smile at the exhausted academic.

'Thanks for the tea.'

Lucinda had been back in her room for about a quarter of an hour when one of the college porters knocked at her door.

'Excuse me, Miss Farrer, but there is a telephone call for you in the lodge.' She hurried back with him to the gateway and went into the porters' lodge and picked up the phone.

'Lucinda? It's me. Jennifer. How are you?'

'Jennifer!' Lucinda was astounded and delighted. 'God, I thought that you were in the wilds of California! Where are you speaking from?'

'I'm back in 'appy 'Ampstead. I flew in today.'

'Is Merton with you?' Lucinda's voice trembled slightly.

'No. The poor dear is in the middle of a new film and couldn't get away. He sends you his love. But when can I see you? I'm dying to have a long gossip and hear what you've been up to.'

'Term has only just started. I won't be able to get away for a few weeks.'

'That's much too long. Why don't I come to Cambridge?'

'That'd be marvellous. I can find you a room. Can you make it this weekend?'

'Expect me tomorrow night.'

Lucinda worked like a demon throughout Friday, preparing her essay for her tutorial with Michael the following Tuesday. The more work she could get through before the arrival of Jennifer, the more time the two of them would have together without distractions. That evening, she was at the station to meet the London train.

Jennifer rushed through the barrier and threw herself into Lucinda's arms.

'Lucinda, you look wonderful! Glowing, radiant. You must be in love.'

Both girls laughed.

'Let me look at you,' Lucinda replied. 'You've got that superb Hollywood suntan. Tell me, are you the same delicious golden brown all over?'

'Wait and see.'

They had a meal in a restaurant and then went back to Lucinda's room in college. They were sitting, sipping coffee; an old Ella Fitzgerald record softly flooded the room with nostalgia. Jennifer stroked Lucinda's hair. Her voice was husky with emotion.

'You don't know how much I've missed you, Lucinda.'

'It's been a long time, Jennifer. I often thought of those days at Hurstmonbury.'

'Will you ever forgive me?'

Lucinda stared at the tall, dark girl, whose hand reached out for her own.

'Forgive you? For what, Jennifer?'

'You were so affectionate. You used to follow me

everywhere. You were calling out for love so desperately and I was too blind to realize what you were going through and I did nothing to respond.'

'You mustn't say that,' Lucinda cried. 'You were sweet; I was the silly one. I was so moonstruck. I must have been a dreadful nuisance.'

Jennifer kissed her tenderly.

'Darling Lucinda, let's see if I can do better now.'

Jennifer's fingers were as soft as gossamer, as she caressed Lucinda. Having Jennifer make love to her took her by surprise and yet seemed so natural, as if it were an inevitable fulfilment of the great love which had smouldered in both of them for so many years. When she had been a starry-eyed schoolgirl, Lucinda had dreamt of letting her hands roam over the body of the girl she worshipped, but now, it was Jennifer who took the initiative.

'Has no woman ever made love to you?'

Lucinda was too aroused to speak: she shook her head. Lucinda closed her eyes. She felt her jeans slipping to the floor and Jennifer's eager fingers removing her panties and sensuously caressing her thighs and buttocks. She gasped at the delicate touch of Jennifer's mouth, kissing and teasing her stomach and exploring the depths of her navel.

Then, the petal touch of her lover's lips was searching through the golden curls between her thighs. The delight was almost unbearable when a hot, lascivious tongue darted from between those lips, seeking out the most secret parts of her womanhood.

She was glowing, wet, warm and it was so sweet, so soft, it should never end. She grabbed Jennifer's head and pressed her face deeper, ever deeper.

'Come into me,' Lucinda moaned, 'Put your tongue into me, all the way.'

Slowly, she sank to the floor. Time vanished. There was simply one eternal moment. Jennifer was lying beside her, her head still between Lucinda's legs. Each time that

50

Jennifer flicked her tongue over her clitoris every nerve in her body thrilled until she felt herself falling into an orgasm which shattered her mind and left her body quivering.

'Sh. Be quiet,' Jennifer whispered.

'Why? What's the matter?'

'You were screaming. You'll have somebody coming in from next door.'

'I didn't know I was making a sound,' Lucinda panted.

'Well, you were, my sweet. Lie quietly for a moment.'

After a minute or two, Lucinda asked, 'Did you come too?'

'Yes, but you were too far gone to notice.'

For a long time, they lay in each other's arms, talking little, happy at having found themselves after so many years. It was as though their lives had been one preparation for that coming together.

The evening wore on without any interruption to their complete happiness. Lucinda could not recall ever having passed so perfect a night. Not merely without a cross word, but in such a profound harmony that it was as if they had become one woman sharing two bodies.

It could not last. Moments of true perfection never can. There comes the time when the coldness of the outside world can no longer be denied. The bubble bursts, the dream ends.

It was in the early hours of the morning that Lucinda told Jennifer that she would have to leave and go to the room which had been reserved for her in the college. Jennifer's face fell.

'Can't I stay here and spend the night with you?'

'I'm afraid not, dear. You see, early in the morning the servants come into the college and if they were to catch somebody in my room, I'd be in terrible trouble.'

'You must be joking.' Jennifer was incredulous.

'I'm serious. There are still very strict and old-fashioned rules here. It's strange really. In some ways we under-graduates are treated as mature adults and in other ways we are still cossetted like children.'

Reluctantly, Jennifer left her lover for the night and slept in a small guest bedroom on an adjoining staircase. Sure enough, she was awakened in the morning by a sour-faced spinster who grudgingly offered her a cup of tea.

The two girls went around the town for the next couple of days and looked in on a few of Lucinda's friends. They made love twice more, always with the same gentle wonder.

'When do you have to be back in London?' Lucinda asked.

'I don't have anything arranged before next Wednesday. Do you think I can stay until then or will that cause problems?'

'No, that'll be all right but I shall have to leave you sometimes when I have work to do.'

So, Jennifer stayed on after the weekend for the extra couple of days.

On the Tuesday evening, Lucinda explained that she had to go to a tutorial with Michael.

'What, this time of night?' Jennifer was astonished.

'It's the only time he has free for me.'

Jennifer thought for a while and then she asked in a flat, calculated tone.

'What sort of a man is this Michael Johnson?'

'Well, as I said, he's a young fellow of the college – very clever.'

'Is he handsome?'

'Since you ask, yes, he's quite a good looking stud.'

Jennifer stared at Lucinda intently.

'Has this Michael made love to you?'

Lucinda said nothing. She did not want to lie to her friend but she did not want to admit to Jennifer how things stood between her and her tutor. It was none of her business.

'Look, Jennifer, I have to go and I don't know how long I shall be. Why don't we call it a night and I'll see you in the morning?'

52

Jennifer nodded and the two of them left the room.

Michael was waiting for her; she walked over and kissed him but he pointed to the armchair.

'First, I want to hear your essay. You are here for a tutorial which, I remind you, you pay for. So let's get down to work.'

His voice was light but he was in earnest; Dutifully, Lucinda opened her notebook and began to read to him the essay which she had prepared. For more than an hour his comments and criticisms were entirely confined to the subject matter of her essay. Then, the work done, he relaxed.

'Would you like a glass of sherry?'

Lucinda shook her head, stood up and reached for her gown.

'Please, don't go.' Michael's voice was urgent.

'I thought that all that interested you was what I had written in my notebook.'

'Don't you understand, Lucinda?' He was pleading with her in his misery. 'It's not that I don't want you. I've thought of nothing else since last Thursday. I've counted the minutes until you were due to walk through that door. But I must be honest with you and give you the same tuition that I would anybody else. As I told you, I'm paid for that and like any workman, I take a pride in my job.'

Lucinda smiled. She could not be cross with him – or, at least, not for long. She put her books down, walked over and kissed his cheek.

'Why don't we go into your bedroom?'

Lucinda ruffled his hair affectionately as Michael tore off his clothes and then turned to undress her.

'No, darling, you are clumsy. I'll do it myself.'

Between the sheets, they made love joyfully. Michael was a good, if rather conventional, lover, but Lucinda set about broadening his experience. She found him an adept pupil and it amused her to think that after receiving an hour's tuition from him it was now her turn to be the teacher and he became her student.

Michael kissed her hungrily and clasped her to him with a passionate earnestness as if he was afraid that she would melt away in his embrace. Lucinda could not help feeling amused. Michael seemed to be confused and want to perform every conceivable act of lovemaking at once and he did not know where to begin. She pressed his head down on to her breast. He kissed her avidly, but she shook her head and said.

'Lick my nipples and suck them.'

Michael looked up at her uncertainly but did as she told him.

'No, no, not so rough. Gently, lovingly. Here, let me show you.'

Lucinda pushed him on to his back and lowered herself on to his eager body. She took his small nipples in her mouth, first one then the other and licked them with long, lascivious strokes of her tongue.

'That's the way to do it. Do you like it?'

Michael nodded and looked up at her.

'But I'd rather do it to you,' he replied hoarsely.

Lucinda lifted her body and then gently allowed one white breast to descend on Michael's feverish lips. As his tongue paid homage to her beauty, Michael felt Lucinda's sweet, young nipples going tense and erect and the sensation excited him.

'Now, go down and do the same thing to me there.'

This too was obviously a novel experience for Michael and Lucinda guided his head until his tongue was in contact with her clitoris.

'Yes, yes, that's better. Not too fast to start with. Gently, gently, Michael, make love to me there.'

Michael thrust his body against Lucinda's long, smooth legs. He needed to feel every inch of her body against his own. Every nerve cried out for her and ached to become

54

part of her. Her juices were drenching him as her own pleasure grew more abandoned and her muscles tautened, gripping his head in a vice like embrace until she came with a wild, throbbing, uncontrollable, explosive climax.

Michael would have gone on caressing her, but she pushed him away. He looked at her doubtingly, almost resentfully. Lucinda smiled at him.

'Don't worry, dear. It's just that I'm sensitive there for the moment. Your turn is coming.'

'I'm sorry, I didn't realize—'

Lucinda took his swollen penis in her hand and stroked the thrusting big, blue vein. Then, firmly and deftly, she slipped it into her soaking wet vagina. Its velvet smoothness gave sweet relief, but Michael's lusting desire was so intense that he was only capable of delivering a few piston strokes before his whole load of hot sperm gushed wildly in a great, viscous stream and fell back, panting and gasping.

'Don't they go in for oral sex in Bradford?' she teased when they were lying, side by side, getting their breath back.

'I haven't slept with every woman in the North Country,' he protested. 'But, for me, you were the first.'

Lucinda grinned. He was such a little boy in some ways. With a sigh, she reached for her clothes.

'Please, Lucinda, don't go. You can stay here for the night. It would make me so happy to see you when I open my eyes in the morning.'

'Michael, you know that I can't stay. There'd be hell to pay if I were found here in the morning.'

'Don't worry, my sweet. I have told my bedder not to call me early tomorrow. Nobody will be around until half-past-eight and that gives you plenty of time to slip out.'

Lucinda giggled. 'You had it all worked out. I suppose you gave him some yarn about having so much work to get through that you did not want to be disturbed.'

'Something like that. Anyway, it is a better story than not

being able to get away from the office. You'll stay?'

Lucinda had a pang of conscience when she thought about Jennifer but then she remembered having told her not to wait. She felt so comfortable, and Michael had a cuddly quality which she was sure would be enhanced as the night passed.

'I haven't brought a nightdress,' she said, her eyes modestly downcast.

'I hardly think that will prove too serious,' Michael laughed.

He woke her at about a quarter-to-eight and she dressed quickly.

'It's been nice here but can we go out somewhere? Perhaps next weekend?' Lucinda put the question quite casually.

But Michael's answer was not casual. He shook his head and a look of pain clouded his features. He hesitated, and then spoke very softly.

'I'm sorry but I have not been honest with you, Lucinda. You see, I am married.'

Lucinda was shaken. She recalled Michael's rather fumbling first efforts at lovemaking with her. She had been so sure that he was a novice. Married? She stared at him.

'I can't believe it. Where is your wife?'

'She is visiting her parents. In Bradford,' he smiled bitterly; 'She'll be back this afternoon. But I do love you, Lucinda. Don't get me wrong.'

'How long have you been married?' Lucinda's voice was cold.

'Just over a year.'

'And you love your wife as well?'

'I thought so. Now, I am not so sure.'

Lucinda pondered. Then, she asked in a controlled voice.

'What do you want to do, Michael? Shall we stop meeting?'

He shook his head.

56

'That wouldn't solve anything. Remember, I am your tutor and awkward questions would be asked if either you or I were to demand a change. No, Lucinda, we have to go on working together and that means seeing each other alone. And you know what that must lead to.'

'And your wife, is she what might be called broad-minded?'

'No way.' Michael was emphatic. 'She comes from a highly conventional family. Her father owns a small grocery shop and they all troop off to chapel every Sunday. Annie is very sweet and she's pretty, but if she thought that I had a mistress, she would have a fit.'

'Do you want to leave her?' Lucinda purposely kept her tone unemotional. She was desperately trying to be objective.

'I don't know. This has all been so sudden. Not yet, anyway, I need time to sort myself out.'

'Does your wife live here?'

'No, of course not. We have a flat in the town but I need rooms in college for tutorials.'

'Very convenient,' Lucinda remarked drily. 'Very well, Michael, if you are not prepared to leave your Annie and we have to go on working together, we'll just have to be very careful.' With a nod to her discomforted lover, Lucinda left.

It was still before eight when Lucinda crept back into her own rooms. She rumpled the bedclothes so that her bedder would not notice that she had not spent the night safely ensconced between her own chaste sheets. That worthy was surprised to find her up and dressed when she arrived, but Lucinda explained that she had risen early since she had a lot of reading to get through before her first lecture. The toast was hot and the coffee steaming, when Jennifer knocked on her door. Lucinda let her in and went to kiss her, but Jennifer turned her face away. She looked pale, and drawn; her mouth was grim and the gaiety of yesterday had vanished from her eyes.

'What's the matter with you?' Lucinda asked. 'You look

as if you have not slept a wink.'

'Why did you do it, Lucinda?' Jennifer breathed.

'Do what?' Lucinda felt her irritation mounting.

'You could not spend the night with me. You sent me off to sleep on my own but when you go to your so-called tutor you can manage. No worry about being found by the servants, there!'

'What do you mean? How do you know?'

'I couldn't sleep, so I came back here in the middle of the night to see if I could get a hot drink. Why, Lucinda? Are you in love with this man?'

'Oh, God, first him, then you,' Lucinda burst out. 'How the hell do I know if I love him? And does it matter?'

'It matters to me.' There was a sadness in Jennifer's voice which Lucinda had never heard before. 'Isn't my love enough for you. Why do you need a man? I thought that you were so happy with me.'

'I was. It was great, but I still need a man. Can't you understand, Jennifer, I am a man's woman. Your father knew that well enough. I want to be with you and to make love to you, but, in the last resort, I need a man – that's just the way I am.'

'And this Michael. He's the man of your dreams, is he? He can give you what I can't?'

There were tears of bitterness and resentment in Jennifer's eyes.

'Yes, dammit,' Lucinda shouted. 'He's wonderful, terrific, sensational. And he's married!'

They glared at each other in silence.

At last, Jennifer spoke.

'So, where does that leave you?'

'What do you mean, where does that leave me? It leaves me having an affair in secret, as though I was ashamed of being his lover.'

'And you are going on seeing him?' Jennifer's voice was tinged with malice and menace.

'Yes, yes, yes!' screamed Lucinda. Her fists were clenched and defiance shone in her eyes.

Jennifer turned away.

'I'm going home. Don't bother to contact me.'

The door closed behind her. Lucinda was panting in rage and annoyance. Jennifer's spite and her appeal had only strengthened her resolve to go on with her clandestine affair with Michael.

It was nearly three weeks later that the blow fell. It seemed innocuous enough. A typed message on a postcard left in her pigeon-hole in the Junior Common Room. 'Please come to see me in my rooms at 4 this afternoon,' it ran and it was signed by H. G. B. Parkinson, PhD.

Tea and buns and a polite enquiry after the health of my dear Mama, thought Lucinda, as she walked across to the rooms of her Moral Tutor.

'Sit down, Miss Farrer.' Dr Parkinson was brisk and businesslike. It was a command, not a request. Lucinda felt a twinge of unease, as she seated herself opposite the elderly Fellow.

His words were direct, his tone abrupt.

'I understand that you are having an affair with Mr Johnson.'

Lucinda was too startled to reply. His eyes were shrewd, cold and hostile. There was no way that she could deceive this man and she knew it. He continued.

'Before you say anything, I might as well tell you that there would be little point in your denying it. I have received statements from witnesses. You have been observed, Miss Farrer. Do I make myself clear?'

Lucinda nodded.

'Observed. But how?'

'That does not concern you. Certain steps were taken when Mrs Johnson received an anonymous letter, accusing her husband and you of misconduct. You did know that Mr Johnson was married, didn't you?'

59

Again, Lucinda nodded.

'The matter is to be considered by my colleagues and myself at a formal meeting tomorrow morning. In case you are in any doubt, let me assure you that we take a serious view of a relationship which we consider calculated to bring discredit upon the college. I can't think of anything that you might want to say in mitigation of your conduct but this is your opportunity. Well, Miss Farrer?'

'There is nothing that I can say,' she replied in a broken voice. 'What, now?'

'Please go back to your own rooms. Do not attempt to make contact with Mr Johnson. He has been asked to stay out of college and I am sure that even you would have more sense than to try to communicate with him at his home.'

Lucinda got to her feet and walked to the door. Her fingers were on the handle when Dr Parkinson called to her.

'Before you go, let me say one thing to you, not as your Moral Tutor, but as a man and a member of this college. I don't give a damn what happens to you. As far as I am concerned, you are just one more spoilt brat with more money than sense. I expect that you will shed a few tears and then find consolation in some other man's bed. But do you realize what you have done to Mr Johnson? He was a young man with a brilliant, academic career before him. He'd got to where he is now by sheer hard work, not because Daddy could buy him a place in some exclusive school. The scandal will ruin him. And that's the end of his life's work while he is still in his twenties – all for a romp between the sheets with a young tart! Do you wonder that I am disgusted?'

'If I tell you that it was all my fault – which it was – can't you take a more lenient view of Mr Johnson's involvement?'

Lucinda's entreaty made little effect.

'I fear that in view of the attitude adopted by Mrs Johnson, such a course will not be open to us. Good day, Miss Farrer, I shall be speaking to you in the morning.'

Lucinda stumbled out of the room and hurried back to

her own rooms. With an effort, she choked back tears of impotent rage. What right had these grey, old men to sit in judgement on her and Michael? They had made love: did that justify treating them as though they were criminals? She was tempted to ignore Dr Parkinson's instructions and to phone Michael but the realization that she might find herself talking to his wife stopped her. His wife, there was the person to blame. Why had she made such a fuss over the affair? Perhaps she was so insecure that she could not stand the prospect of her husband looking at another woman. Anyway, what sort of a person was this Mrs Johnson? She must have thought about the consequences of complaining to the college authorities, what it would mean to Michael's future.

Lucinda's brain was awhirl with anger and wounded pride but she experienced something close to panic when she considered how her own parents would react to the disgrace of whatever disciplinary action the college would take against her. Alone in her room, her self control finally gave way and tears flooded down her face. Sobbing hysterically, she flung herself onto her bed and abandoned herself to the violence of her emotions.

Gradually her outburst subsided, leaving her in a sort of numbed state of shock and despair. Somehow, she had to pass the eternity of that night before she would know what punishment would be meted out to her and to Michael by those hard faced, unsympathetic guardians of the college morals.

She had never experienced a night as wretched as that one. She tried to read but the words made no sense. Neither the radio nor the TV could distract her. She felt utterly alone: there was nobody in the world in whom she could confide or to whom she could look for comfort. Inside her room, she felt confined and oppressed, so she wandered out and walked through the busy streets of the town.

Her mind was a blank, her only sensation the nagging

question what was to become of her and Michael in the morning. She knew that she ought to eat something and she drifted into a restaurant and ordered a meal. But when the food arrived, she had no appetite and she left the food untouched on her plate. Disconsolately, she walked into a pub and bought herself a drink. She had hoped that she would find some relief in the warm, good humoured company of the young men and women, chattering and joking, but she felt excluded from their happiness and, more alone and vulnerable than ever, she slunk out of the pub and back to the quiet gloom of her own rooms in college.

She could not rest but, after she had taken a valium, she eventually fell into a fitful sleep as sheer exhaustion blunted the acuteness of her misery. But slumber brought her no relief. Her anguish and anxiety haunted her: no sedative would have been strong enough to dispel them. She tossed and turned in her bed as she experienced a nightmare of such vivid clarity that even after she had awakened she was not able to dismiss it from her mind.

She and Michael were standing before the assembled senior members of the college. They were all dressed in fantastic, mediaeval robes as if they were officials of the Inquisition while Michael and she were naked. She wanted to cover herself from the derisive, sneering regard of her tormentors, but she was unable to move her hands. They were speaking to her but she could not hear their words. Yet, she knew what they were saying and every time their lips moved in silent condemnation, her body was wracked by terrible pain. She looked over to Michael and saw that his body was writhing in agony as flames engulfed him. He was screaming: she could see his lips moving but was not able to hear a sound. His body was turning brown and charred before her eyes but his silent screams never ceased. She turned her gaze back at her pitiless judges. Every eye was on her, unblinking, never wavering for a second. She felt herself withering, shrinking, her guilt exposed for all to

62

see. She knew that she had to suffer. Her legs were being forced open and the scorching fire was thrusting itself inside her, destroying her womb, burning out what was unclean. Her own screaming woke her.

In the morning, she awaited the summons from Dr Parkinson, sick with anxiety and foreboding. She watched her fellow students hurrying off to lectures or to the libraries, as if they were characters in a film. They were no more part of her life than the shadows which she would watch on the screen in a cinema. She did not know how long she had been sitting at the window. Time had lost its meaning. There was a knock at her door.

'Miss Farrer,' one of the college porters had stuck his head around the door. 'Dr Parkinson sends his compliments and would like to see you now.'

As if in a trance, Lucinda got to her feet and draped her gown over her shoulders. She followed the burly porter out into the Court.

'No, Miss, this way, please.'

He was not leading her to the rooms of Dr Parkinson, but over to the opposite corner of the Great Court and Lucinda realized with a shock that she was being escorted to the sober façade of the Master's Lodge. The last, lingering hope that the whole business could be quietly buried, disappeared. An interview with the Master of Trinity was not the occasion for a simple reprimand.

She found herself in the presence of the Master and Dr Parkinson. This time, nobody invited her to take a seat.

'Miss Farrer, let's not waste time.' The Master's voice went through her like steel. 'You know the reason that we have called for you. You might care to see this.'

He passed her a piece of notepaper. It bore the college crest and she read the typed message, a simple letter from Michael to the Master, resigning his fellowship.

Lucinda handed the letter back without a word.

'Under the circumstances, we have no alternative but to accept Mr Johnson's resignation.'

Lucinda found her voice.

'I explained to Dr Parkinson yesterday that the whole thing is my fault. Do you have to be so severe on Mr Johnson?'

'You ought to know that Mrs Johnson is suing for divorce. Mr Johnson really had no alternative to tendering his resignation which we feel obliged to accept.'

Lucinda dropped her eyes and awaited the inevitable.

'I am sure that you would not be happy to continue your studies here. Be so kind as to visit the Bursar this afternoon and he will present you with your account. It would be appropriate if you were to leave Cambridge this evening. Thank you, Miss Farrer, that will be all.'

Lucinda found herself back in her rooms. She had no recollection of walking across the Court. She took down her case and mechanically started to pack her things.

Sitting in the London train, Lucinda's brain began to function again. She had been so overwhelmed by her feelings of anger and distress that she had not stopped to speculate on who had brought down these disasters on Michael and herself. Now she wanted to solve that mystery, to find out who was responsible and to seek revenge. She gritted her teeth: she could kill whoever had been so vile as to ruin them.

What was it that Dr Parkinson had said? Somebody had sent an anonymous letter to Michael's wife and that had started the whole sordid business of spying on them and their disgrace. The two of them had only met in Michael's rooms and she was certain that there had been no opportunity for the writer to have seen them in bed together. Once the college authorities had been warned, they had almost certainly arranged to have Michael's rooms observed from the windows of another room opposite but it seemed inconceivable that the occupant was the writer of the anonymous letter. What possible motive would he have had? No, it must have come from somebody who had been told that they were having an affair and was jealous of one or other of the lovers.

Suddenly, she knew. As soon as her train pulled into Liverpool Street station, Lucinda placed her case in the Left Luggage and found a taxi. Climbing in, she gave the driver the address of Merton's flat in Hampstead.

It was mid-afternoon, when she arrived. Jennifer was alone in the apartment. When she opened the door to Lucinda, her face registered astonishment and something else. Could it have been fear?

'Lucinda, what are you doing here?'

Lucinda's eyes were as hard as diamonds, her mouth grim, as she pushed her way into the flat. She wheeled round on Jennifer.

'It was you, wasn't it?'

'What are you talking about?'

'Don't try playing the innocent with me. You were the one who sent that letter to Michael's wife.'

Jennifer stood very still and said nothing.

'Why, Jennifer, why? Were you so madly jealous? I've been sent down and Michael has been forced to resign his fellowship. He's ruined.'

All at once, Jennifer flared up.

'Yes, damn you, of course I sent the letter. I found out the address of your boy friend's wife from the porter of your college: I said that I wanted to send her some flowers. So, you're being sent down – that's the same as being expelled isn't it? Good! I'm glad, glad, do you hear? How do you think I felt when you rejected my love to stay with that man?'

All her pent-up rage seemed to come to the boil and Lucinda sprang at the girl whom she had loved so passionately.

'You fucking bitch,' she screamed, 'I'll tear you to pieces!'

Before Jennifer could do anything to defend herself,

Lucinda had grabbed her by the hair and was forcing her head back. Jennifer uttered a cry of pain and fell heavily over a small table. In an instant, both girls were rolling on the floor, biting, scratching and pummelling each other. Lucinda would not let go of Jennifer's hair and she tugged until she yanked out great tufts by the root. Jennifer made a grab at Lucinda's eyes but just missed. Her nails raised red weals down Lucinda's cheek and blood started to trickle from her nose.

'I'll kill you! I'll kill you!' Lucinda screeched. Then she gasped in pain, as Jennifer smashed her knee up into her groin.

There was a crash, as the struggling, sweating, cursing pair of wild, young animals knocked over a cabinet. They ignored the splintering of wood and the shattered glass.

'What in heaven's name is going on?'

Merton had entered unheard, and was gazing in astonishment at the wild scene. Neither girl answered but Lucinda unsteadily climbed to her feet. She had no quarrel with Merton but she could not collect herself sufficiently to speak to him. Shaking her head like a wounded beast, she straightened her torn clothes and, without a word, let herself out of the flat.

Part 2

5

The Honourable Miles Farrer, future sixteenth Viscount Hamblewood, glanced irritably at his watch. The damned trains were always late. He was busy and really could not spare the time, but somebody had to go to the station and meet Lucinda and help with the mountain of luggage.

I don't supporse that she has changed, Miles thought. She had been a shallow, selfish, sex-crazed child when she had brought disgrace to that young tutor and had been thrown out of Cambridge so ignominiously. The family had been too ashamed to parade her around England and she had been sent to spend a couple of years at an elegant Swiss 'finishing school'. She has probably learnt how to wear a big picture hat and long white gloves so that she can float around fashionable garden parties or get into the glossy pages of those snob magazines which cover the doings of high society, reflected her brother. Well, he would soon know: twenty minutes behind schedule, the London train was pulling into the station, bringing Lucinda back to her ancestral home.

For a moment, he did not recognize her. The Cambridge undergraduate had been little more than a child, dressed in blue jeans and sweat shirt, with her hair carelessly tied back. What he now saw, was a trim, young woman, smartly dressed in a navy blue dress with matching shoes and handbag. Her hair was carefully arranged, her make up discreet, not a hair out of place. Miles was agreeably surprised by this display of modesty and good taste. Perhaps Switzerland had done something for her after all.

Lucinda spotted Miles as she walked out of the station, escorted by a porter pushing a trolley piled high with her cases. He appeared as pallid and as dull as the day she had left.

'Miles, I do believe that you are going bald!'

He raised a hand to his forehead and scowled.

'Nonsense. My hair is as healthy as ever. What a way to greet me – welcome home, sister!'

'Don't be offended, my dear. It's supposed to be a sign of virility.'

Miles' expression made it clear that he did not regard Lucinda's observation as a compliment. The luggage was stowed into the car and they drove back to Hamblewood in almost total silence.

Her father's embrace was absent-minded and her mother's lukewarm. It was as though she had never been away and the shame and humiliation of her departure from Cambridge still rankled.

For a few days, Lucinda moped about the house, vainly trying to find something to interest her. Then, a chance encounter changed the whole course of her life.

Her mother had to go to London for a meeting of a committee on which she served and she offered to take Lucinda with her. While the Viscountess went off to her meeting, Lucinda took the opportunity to go shopping and arranged to meet her mother at the Belgrave Square flat, where they would spend the night. The shops were closing for the evening and Lucinda was tired from her expedition but she did not feel like going straight home. She had lunched early and, she fancied a snack. There was a small café a few yards along Kensington High Street where she had eventually found herself and she went inside.

It was a noisy, crowded, self-service restaurant and Lucinda was jostled in a queue which moved past the trays of unappetizing dead sandwiches and burnt offerings. She selected a few of the less revolting items, paid her bill and searched for somewhere to sit. She found the last free table and gratefully put down her tray and sank into a hideously

70

uncomfortable, plastic chair. Almost immediately, a young woman fought her way to the table. She was carrying a tray on which were piled a limp salad, a sausage roll of dubious origin and a cup of hot liquid which was sold as coffee.

'Do you mind if I sit at your table? There's no other place free.'

Lucinda waved at the chair opposite her: the girl set down her tray and dropped into the chair.

'My God, how my feet ache!'

She was a girl of about Lucinda's own age with long, ash blonde hair. Her eyes were light brown with a few strange, golden flecks which matched the faint freckles on her face. She had a good humoured smile and an open, frank expression as if she would open her heart to anyone who would listen. She unbuttoned her jacket, revealing well shaped, firm breasts and a trim, yet athletic, figure. Lucinda took an instant liking to her and was ready for a few minutes' conversation with this pleasant looking stranger. And the girl was certainly not shy.

'Have you been walking far?' Lucinda asked.

'I've been rushing about practically the whole day, trying to find somewhere to live; have you any idea how difficult it is for a girl on her own to find a room or a studio in London?'

Lucinda shook her head.

'And being a bloody foreigner doesn't help,' her companion continued. 'Tell me, why is it that for the English there are no ordinary foreigners, only bloody foreigners? I'm Australian myself – you probably spotted the accent and the name is Sarah Brown.'

'I'm Lucinda Farrer.'

'Lucinda. That's a funny name. Are you English?'

'Yes, but don't worry. I've only just got back to England myself, so I am quite used to bloody foreigners.'

Sarah laughed. 'I suppose I must sound a dreadful moaner. The fact is that I only landed in England a few days

71

ago and I've really had a hell of a job, settling down. First of all, I had to find a job. I was lucky. A girl friend of mine back in Sydney gave me the name of a fellow over here who's a big shot in some company or other. I called him up and he told me to come over. Next thing I knew, I had a job starting next Monday. Well, that was one worry less, but I then had to find somewhere to live. Of course, I wanted to get it fixed up before I start work while I have got time to go and see places. I managed to find a flat this afternoon: nothing grand, just a couple of rooms in Chelsea.'

'You've done very well. All that in a couple of days.'

'Well, it's been a week, actually. There are plenty of flats advertised. Finding one is no problem. But paying for one is a different matter. Everything is so expensive. You know when I've paid the rent and my fare on the Tube to work, I'll barely have enough left of my pay to afford one meal a day.'

'And you honestly couldn't find anywhere cheaper?'

'You must be joking. No, I was getting desperate. I've been staying in a small hotel and I really had to get out before I ran out of money, so I agreed to take this place but what I want is to find another girl to move in with me and split the cost.'

They chatted on, and Sarah told Lucinda all about the flat. As well as the two rooms, it had its own kitchen and was decently furnished. It had a phone and was in a quiet side street off the King's Road near to Sloane Square.

'Sounds ideal,' said Lucinda, preparing to leave. 'You should be able to find somebody to share without too much trouble.'

'Yes, it is nice. It's a pity I don't have any friends over here. If you happen to know a girl who is looking for a place, you might send her along. Here, I'll give you the address and the phone number.'

Sarah pulled out a piece of paper and scribbled on it.

'Thanks,' said Lucinda, stuffing the paper into her bag. 'I

don't know anybody right now, but if I do come across a likely girl, I'll get her to contact you. Meanwhile, the best of luck with the job; I hope that everything turns out OK.'

'Thank you Luc— what did you say your name was?'

'Lucinda. Ciao.'

Back in Hamblewood, Lucinda forgot all about Sarah Brown. She had other things on her mind. First and foremost was Franz.

She had never expected him to write but there was this postcard waiting for her. You can't get much on a postcard but Franz had succeeded in conveying two messages. First, that he missed Lucinda and the good times that they had together. Secondly, he was taking a few days' vaction and he would like to come to England and stay with Lucinda.

Of course, Miles had read the postcard and disapproved.

'Now what sort of a creature have you picked up?' he wanted to know. 'We thought that you were safe in Switzerland but we ought to have known that you would get yourself into some sort of trouble. Who is this Franz – an ancient gigolo who has his eye on your money?'

Lucinda stamped her foot in annoyance.

'How dare you read my private correspondence?'

'I think that you had better tell us something about this Franz, dear,' her mother interposed quietly.

'He's about twenty and he's Swiss,' Lucinda replied, swallowing her fury. 'Miles has an evil mind. Franz is just an ordinary guy.'

'But you are not just an ordinary girl,' her mother persisted. 'What more do you know about him?'

Lucinda knew a great deal, but she did not think that it would be a good idea to share her intimate recollections with her family.

She had first met Franz one Saturday afternoon in an ice cream parlour in Geneva. Although discipline in the finishing school was strict, the young ladies were allowed a few hour's freedom during the weekends. Everybody would make a dash into Geneva to meet friends, go to a cinema, have a decent meal in a restaurant or simply feel that they were away from the restrictions of the school for a few hours.

Lucinda was sitting with one of her school friends, a serious looking Swedish girl, rather plain and unexciting but intelligent and good company. Franz served them with an air of friendliness. Lucinda looked at him carefully. He was definitely the best looking waiter in the joint.

Business was slack and Franz loitered by their table, happy to have the chance to gossip with a couple of girls and break the boredom.

'Why are there so few people here on a Saturday?'

'It's such fine weather. Everybody gets out of town, up in the hills or out on the lake. That's where I'd be if this were my day off. What do you girls do for a living?'

Before her companion could say that they were at school, Lucinda put in hastily.

'We work for one of the banks. We are both in the typing pool.'

'God, that must be even more boring than being a waiter,' Franz commiserated. 'Say, do you like dancing?'

'No,' said the Swede.

'Yes,' said Lucinda.

'Would you like to come with me when I've finished here this evening? We could go to the Gallipoli. Do you know it, the new disco near the Richemond? It's all decorated in Turkish style and it's where all the youngsters in this God-forsaken city go.'

'No,' said the Swede.

'What time do you finish?' asked Lucinda.

'I'll be through at ten-thirty.'

'I'll see you here. But I won't be able to stay out late. We have rooms just out of town and our landlady is a dragon. If I came crawling back at some unearthly hour in the morning, she would throw me out as soon as look at me.'

'Well, just stay for an hour or two.'

Franz hurried off to serve a couple of customers who had come in while they were talking. The moment he was out of earshot, the Swedish girl turned to Lucinda in shocked confusion.

'What do you think you are doing? Why did you tell that young man that we were typists? And how could you agree to meet him when you know that you have to be back in school by ten-thirty?'

'If I had said that we were still at school, that would have put him off, especially if he knew which school. He'd be scared stiff of us. And as for getting back, it'll be all right. When you get into school, you can sign me in without anybody noticing. I'll be back in time for the roll call in the morning, I promise.'

'But how will you get in?'

'Oh, don't be silly. I can climb over the wall. I've done it hundreds of times. Don't worry: just promise to sign the book tonight.'

All went according to plan. Before Lucinda left Franz for her own brand of mountaineering, she had promised to see him again the following week.

The next Saturday was Franz's day off and they met after lunch. He led Lucinda down to the lakeside and pointed to a tiny sailing dinghy, bobbing in the waves.

'That's my boat. Let me take you for a sail.'

'Do you get paid enough as a waiter to have a boat?'

'It's only a little boat,' Franz protested, 'and I saved every cent I earned for a couple of years. The other boys who work with me went off on charter trips to Spain or Greece each summer but I stayed at home and used the money for that instead.'

Lucinda smiled at his obvious pride in the diminutive, white painted craft, just big enough for a couple of people.

'I know,' she said, 'let's have a picnic. We can buy some bread and cheese and fruit and take a bottle of wine.'

'Great!' Franz enthused. 'I know a perfect spot on the

lake. It's quite close but somehow nobody ever goes there. It's a bit tucked away and people don't notice it, especially if they go rushing past in speedboats.'

It took them less than half an hour to buy the provisions and cast off and after about an hour's sailing, Franz steered the boat into a tiny inlet. The entrace was screened by low, overhanging branches from the trees which lined the lake and they had to let down the sail before they slipped through into a small, natural basin.

Although they were sheltered from the direct rays of the blazing sun, it was very warm. They ate their food and drank some of the wine. Franz leaned back, contentedly and took off his shirt.

Lucinda regarded the young man. He was about nineteen and had a fresh, out of doors complexion. His short, blond hair was brushed back and it lay in rich curls. He must have been getting out quite a lot, since his chest was well tanned to a deep brown. His muscles rippled as he stretched and relaxed in the idyllic, summer weather.

'What's a nice, English girl doing as a copy typist in a Geneva bank?' he asked.

'Oh, I'm only here for a short time. I was able to arrange the job because the bank was short of typists who were really fluent in English. I'd been over here on a hitch-hiking holiday and I met a guy who told me about it. So, I took a chance and called up the bank and asked for a temporary job. I got an interview and, well, here I am.'

Franz looked longingly at the water.

'It's so hot: I'm going in for a swim. Are you coming, Lucinda?'

'I haven't brought a costume.'

'It doesn't matter here. I told you, nobody ever comes to this spot. Forget the good people of Geneva and let yourself go.'

Franz got to his feet and watching Lucinda, steadfastly and boldly, slowly removed his trousers and brief pants. He

76

stood before her, naked as if daring her to look at his sturdy body and admire his maleness. Lucinda felt herself stirred by this display, this challenge. She pulled off her own clothes and faced Franz, confident in the beauty of her own body.

He touched her arm and with a wicked smile said,

'First, we swim.'

The water was chilly and they plunged about energetically in the lake but after about ten minutes, Lucinda pulled herself on to the bank, shivering. Franz came to her and, taking a towel, rubbed her body until she glowed all over. Then, without a word, he kissed her, first on the lips, then on the breast and finally buried his lips in her crotch.

She looked down on his head which glowed golden in the bright sunshine. He climbed to his feet and her towel fluttered from her shoulders to the ground as he took her in his arms. She felt the warmth of his skin and his keen, young body enfolded her. Lucinda looked up at his handsome, smiling features and first kissed his throat then nibbled his chin. There was the faintest trace of stubble where he had shaved which prickled against her tongue. Despite his plunge in the lake, his skin was salty from his sweat. It was a pleasant taste on her lips, like the smell of his body, tangy but not disagreeably strong.

The lush, green grass, the calm blue water of the lake and the brilliant sun in the cloudless sky, all seemed to be inviting them to make joyful love.

Lucinda closed her eyes. Franz's skin rippled beneath the restless play of her fingers. She felt the firmness of his tongue, hot and hard, as he forced it deep into her, filling her mouth, possessing her. She reached down and took his balls in her hand. They were tight, eager for her, as was his rocklike, probing penis. She felt her own oozing dampness and she knew that she was ready for him.

It was all so simple and natural. There was none of the frenzy of making love to Merton or the impish delight which she took in seducing Michael. She did not love Franz, but

77

sex was easy and good with him. He smelt clean and fresh after the swim and his skin, chilled by the water and then warmed by the embrace of the sun, thrilled to her touch. He felt good inside her and they moved together with one rhythm as if they had been lovers for years. He held her very tight and their mouths sought each other avidly. Franz was moving quicker, his muscles tautening and his breathing getting heavier and more spasmodic. Lucinda could sense that he was nearing his climax and that excited her more. Her whole body seemed to be throbbing uncontrollably. She was exploding: her fingers dug deep into his skin and she was biting his tongue which was pressing deeper and deeper into her mouth. His last furious lunge seemed to take the whole of him into her and she gripped him in a vice-like clasp as she took his wildly jerking and threshing body, and her own orgasm shook her in one moment of complete fulfilment and then of intense relief. Franz collapsed and lay inside her, gasping for breath and sobbing quietly. She stroked his head and he gradually relaxed.

It was too cold to swim again and Lucinda was conscious of the smell of Franz still on her own body and the sensation of his sperm within her, as they sailed back to Geneva and it gave her a sort of second thrill.

They went back to the isolated spot on the lakeside several more times before Lucinda left for England. She had told Franz that she had to go home for family reasons and he had taken her address, promising faithfully to write. Of course. Lucinda was sure that she was just a passing episode in the love life of Franz who would be forgotten a couple of days after they had parted. The last thing that she had expected was a passionate message from him delivered before the scrutiny of her parents and Miles on an all too legible postcard.

No, it would not be advisable to tell them all that she knew about Franz. But what right had they to condemn him when they knew nothing about him. Lucinda shook with fury.

78

'You are not seriously considering inviting this Franz, whoever he may be, to spend his holiday here?'

Miles' tone suggested that the whole Hamblewood clan might contract leprosy, if not worse, were they to even set eyes on the writer of Lucinda's plaintive postcard.

Up to that moment, Lucinda had not thought of taking up Franz's proposition that they spend some time together in England. Now, she was resolute.

'When I was in his country, Franz was a good friend to me; It would be shameful if I could not entertain him for a few days.'

'Just how good a friend was he?' Miles wanted to know.

Before Lucinda could reply, her mother interrupted.

'What exactly does this young man do for a living, dear?'

Viscount Hamblewood made one of his rare utterances.

'He either makes chocolate or cuckoo clocks. They all do in Switzerland - except for the bankers. He isn't by any chance a banker, is he, Lucinda?'

Hope gleamed in the peer's moist eyes. But only for a second.

'He's a waiter,' hissed Lucinda.

The worst fears of the family were confirmed. It was Miles who broke the stupified silence and spoke up for the honour of the Hamblewoods.

'Please write to your gentleman friend and explain that it would not be appropriate for him to be received here.'

Lucinda turned to her mother and father.

'Do you agree with Miles? Are you such snobs that you won't allow poor Franz in the house?'

'Sorry, Lucinda, it's just not on,' her father intoned.

'It would be dreadfully inconvenient,' purred her mother. 'You must remember, dear, that we have so many social engagements coming along. I mean to say, you would not take a waiter to Goodwood or Ascot, would you? And just think of the Buckingham Palace Garden Parties. Really,

79

Lucinda, you must start to consider your position in society.'

'Fuck you, fuck your garden parties and your society! You and all phonies!' Lucinda screamed. Her eyes were blazing but she had to force back tears of exasperation.

Her family were frozen by her outburst. Then, her mother spoke with hard, calculated restraint.

'Lucinda, you will please go to your room and do not return until you have regained control over your temper.'

They stood, looking at her, immobile as models in a waxworks. Lucinda stormed out of the room. As she was passing the phone which stood on a small table at the foot of the stairs, an idea flashed into her head. She ran to her room and rummaged in her bag until she found a scrap of paper. Gripping it in her hand, she hurried back to the phone and dialled the number written on the paper.

The phone was ringing for a few seconds, then a girl answered.

'Hello. Is that Sarah Brown?' Lucinda's voice trembled.

'Yes. Who's that?'

'It's Lucinda. Remember, we met the other day and you asked if I could find somebody to share your flat with you?'

'Oh, yes,' Sarah's tone warmed. 'Say, how are you getting along?'

'Never mind me for the moment. Tell me, have you found anybody yet or are you still looking?'

'Not yet. But I've put a card in a tobacconist's shop around the corner. Seems that's what everyone does. But I only put it in this morning so it's too soon to see how it works out.'

'How about me?'

'What do you mean, Lucinda?'

'Would you take me as a flat-mate? I'd pay my share of everything. How about it?'

'Sure, I'd love that. But I thought that you were all set to stay with your folks somewhere in the country.'

'There's been a change of plan. When can I come?'

'Any time you like. I'll go and take the card out of the tobacconist's window.'

'See you this afternoon.'

Lucinda hung up and raced back upstairs to her room. It took her about ten minutes to throw some clothes and toilet things into a case.

She called a taxi and when it arrived, she left the house without another word to Miles or her parents.

Lucinda was to learn much of life, love and death before she was next to walk into the spacious entrance hall of Hamblewood.

6

Lucinda settled down happily enough in the Chelsea flat. Sarah was an easy-going, if rather untidy, flat-mate. She would rush off to work after gulping down a plate of cornflakes and scrambling into her clothes with the frantic haste of a quick-change artist. Lucinda led a rather more leisurely existence, cleaning up the apartment and doing the shopping.

When she had quit home, Lucinda had some money left from her allowance but she did not want to accept the humiliation of asking her parents for help when that was exhausted. For the first time in her life, Lucinda was looking for a job.

She answered several advertisements and went for a couple of interviews, but without success. Then, one evening, Sarah said to her,

'Lucinda, you were at school in Switzerland, weren't you?'

'That's right, near Geneva.'

'Then you speak pretty good French?'

Lucinda nodded.

'Well, look love, I'll tell you what. You know I've only been in my job for a few weeks but I get along OK and my boss, a guy called Alastair Grant, he's easy to get on with.'

'So, what's that got to do with my speaking French?'

'Alastair has some business in France. I don't know much about it except he goes to Paris quite a bit and I know that he has a French partner. Sometimes he needs to write formal business letters in French. His regular secretary is going on holiday for a couple of weeks and I know that he is looking for a 'temp'. Would you like me to put a word in for you?'

'It would be great, but I am no typist. I belong to the two finger brigade.'

Sarah laughed, 'Don't worry. If you can draft the letters and help with the spelling, I can knock them out on a typewriter in no time. How about it?'

'If you think that you can swing it for me—' Lucinda started but then Sarah interrupted,

'Oh, but I forgot, won't you be wanting to stay at home to look after your boy friend?'

'What boy friend?'

'This waiter you told me about. Isn't he coming over specially to see you?'

'Oh, Franz. He's not my boy friend. At least, not a regular boy friend, if you know what I mean. And as for his coming to England, nothing has been arranged. No, you go ahead and see if you can get me the job at your place.'

The truth was that since she had left Hamblewood in such a dramatic fashion, Lucinda had barely given a thought to the young man who had been the unknowing cause of her break with her family. She realized that she had no great desire to see him and certainly was not willing to disrupt the routine of her life so as to be his escort, day and night, in London. What had made her so determined had been the blind opposition of her family and, without that stimulus, her enthusiasm for her former lover evaporated.

And that was how Lucinda came to meet Alastair Grant.

Lucinda had imagined that she would be working in one of those huge office blocks with hundreds of other people, all part of some mammoth enterprise, but she was agreeably surprised. Alastair's business was conducted from a small suite of offices in a dignified Victorian mansion in the West End. The total staff was about half a dozen and although there was a telex discreetly tucked away in the corner of one of the rooms and a few filing cabinets and typewriters, there was none of the hectic activity which Lucinda associated with commerce.

But Alastair had a genuine business and Lucinda found herself drafting letters, mainly dealing with the running of some properties in France – letters to lawyers, estate agents, banks and to Alastair's partner, Yves Richepin.

As for Alastair himself, even at first meeting, he made a striking impression on her. She followed Sarah into his private office and looked across a stylish steel and rose-wood desk at her first boss.

He was a tall gaunt man in his mid-thirties. He had smooth, black hair, parted in the middle and glittering sharp eyes like those of some bird of prey. This similarity was heightened by his thin beak-like nose and tight lips. But Alastair was not an unattractive man. Just as Merton had exuded a sense of the great actor, everything about Alastair gave expression to a feeling of power – a man capable of swift, decisive action.

However, Alastair was pleasant enough to Lucinda. He spoke to her in French, fluent but with that awkward turn of phrase of a man speaking a foreign language. When she answered in perfect, idiomatic French which she had been speaking for the past few years, he smiled in satisfaction and told her that she was hired.

The work was not too demanding and Lucinda enjoyed her spell in the office. The days soon passed and Lucinda was sorry when one Friday afternoon she put her things away

83

for the last time: Alastair's regular secretary was due back on the following Monday.

She went with Sarah to say goodnight and Alastair thanked her politely but formally for the time she had spent there. As the girls were on the point of leaving, he looked up and said,

'Lucinda, I would like to end our relationship on a pleasant note. If you and Sarah are not doing anything special tonight, would you both like to have dinner with me?'

They agreed and Alastair arranged to pick them up later from their flat. Sarah was excited.

'You know, he's never suggested a date before and I'd really like to get to know him better. Gee, I guess if I make a break-through with Alastair, I'll owe it to you, Lucinda.'

'Let's wait and see how it works out,' Lucinda advised her.

In fact, it worked out very well, although not at all as Sarah would have predicted – or desired. Alastair took them to a trendy, little restaurant in a rambling, rebuilt and redecorated house in Islington, patronized by some celebrated show-biz people and their inevitable hangers-on. However, the food and wine were very good and Alastair proved to be a charming host. Although they chatted throughout the meal, Lucinda learnt practically nothing about him since he had a knack of getting the girls to talk about themselves and he seemed to enjoy hearing about their adventures and their families. They had finished their coffee when Sarah excused herself and, as she put it, went to powder her nose. Alastair leaned over and spoke softly to Lucinda.

'I would hate to think that this will be our last time together. If I contact you in the next few days, would you come out with me again – this time, just the two of us?'

Lucinda was caught off balance. She had not expected for one moment that Alastair would want to see her again but she realized that she liked the prospect.

'I suppose it will be all right. But what about Sarah?'

'What about Sarah? I get along well with her in the office but that does not oblige me to take her out whenever I want to see you, does it?'

'Well, no, not if you put it that way. But I think that she will be terribly disappointed.'

'Disappointed? Perhaps you mean jealous. I wouldn't want to make her unhappy, so why don't we simply make this our little secret? I can call you when she is in the office and I'll give you my private number.'

By the time that Sarah had rejoined them at the table, they were talking about the latest musical to hit the West End stage.

Four days later, Lucinda went out with Alastair, having told Sarah that a cousin had arrived unexpectedly in town. This time, Alastair made no attempt to hide his intentions.

'Finish your Crêpes Suzette and we'll go back to my flat.'

'Sarah is expecting me back.'

'Then call her and tell her not to wait up for you.'

God, he's sure of himself, Lucinda thought. But she went to the phone and called Sarah.

'Oh, it's that sort of cousin,' Sarah laughed. 'Enjoy yourself. I'll see you when you get back – tomorrow I expect. But I insist that you give me a blow by blow account afterwards.'

Alastair's flat was small but sensational. Situated on the twentieth floor of a modern block, it commanded a spectacular view over Hyde Park and the whole of the great, sprawling mass of London to the south for miles to the hazy, half discernible slopes of the beginnings of the Downs. When Lucinda arrived, all that was visible was an infinity of twinkling lights.

The lounge was furnished in modern style, dominated by a gleaming cocktail cabinet. The bedroom was a much more elaborate affair. One wall was taken up by a huge window with that breathtaking view. The others were a lurid scarlet, as was the shiny satin bedcover. To add a more dramatic touch, the ceiling was made up of angled mirrors, all focusing on the bed. And what a bed! An enormous, circular affair with black satin sheets. Lucinda cast an enquiring glance at Alastair.

'It comes in useful when I have a crowd,' he explained.

Alastair gripped her by the wrist and pulled her to him. His kiss was not so much passionate as masterful, as if with his lips he would impose his will on her.

'I adore beautiful, submissive women.' His voice was hard and cold. Lucinda shivered and retorted, 'I've never been submissive.'

'You will be.'

Alastair removed her clothes with a purposefulness which would not be denied, leaving her in her panties and bra. Then, with the same deliberate movements, he laid her on the bed and stretched her arms out above her head. From the lower part of the bed, he pulled out leather straps which ended in loops into which he slipped her wrists. It was so sudden that Lucinda made no attempt to struggle and within seconds her ankles were similarly secured. She lay there, spread-eagled, helpless.

'Don't be frightened. I don't get a kick out of hurting women.'

He towered above her and she gazed up at him, hypnotized. She had no idea what to expect. His hands roamed at will over her body. She wanted to pull away, but she was powerless to stir. Despite his reassuring words, Lucinda was afraid, not so much of what he might do to her as from not knowing what was going to happen. It was the unknown that filled her with apprehension.

'What are you going to do to me?' she murmured.

Alastair replied sardonically, 'I shall do whatever I please. And you will accept it. I told you: you will submit.'

Lucinda was unable to take her eyes off him as he stood erect, dominating her prostrate body, playing with her with malicious casualness.

'And what is more, my pretty, little Lucinda, before I have finished, you will desire to submit. You will beg me to allow you to become my slave.'

His words inflamed her. She wanted to hate Alastair and what he was doing to her but she could feel welling up inside her, even as he spoke, a wild enjoyment of her subjection. She ached to take him in her hands but, being forced to receive caresses without being able to respond physically was unexpectedly exciting. Never in her life had she been so completely vulnerable, so completely at the mercy of another human being.

Deliberately, he drew his thumbnail across her bare breast. It felt hard, menacing but the pressure was not enough to hurt. She felt her body tensing: it would have been less of a torture if he had actually inflicted real pain but all of his actions were charged with a threat of potential suffering yet he never allowed her the relief of pain. She was constantly waiting, fearing and with every second, becoming more and more excited. Alastair had opened his flies and he drew his hard penis over her taut stomach. She felt her juices flowing and she realized that instead of pulling away, she was straining up to be in contact with his masculinity which seemed to be both mocking and mastering her.

Alastair was aware that she could no longer resist and that she had lost the will to struggle against his domination. Slowly, he moved over her and then, very deliberately, lowered his balls on to her mouth. She kissed them passionately, gratefully, but he immediately pulled away again.

'Please, Alastair!' she pleaded pitifully.

Without a word, he thrust his penis into her craving mouth. She took every inch of it and sucked it as if her life depended on her giving her master the maximum pleasure. But Alastair did not allow himself to lose control and again he withdrew.

'Please, please, take me, now!'

But Alastair went on stroking, petting, rubbing her flesh, tormenting her to the point of insanity but, as he had promised, never hurting her. Then, when she had been reduced to hopeless moaning entreaties, he suddenly tore off her last vestiges of her clothing, quickly removed his own clothes and plunged his long, erect penis into her. It was such a relief that she came almost immediately and in the middle of her spasms, she felt the spurting sperm impregnating her.

They relaxed for a moment and then, without a word, Alastair released her from her bonds. She moved down the bed and took him in her mouth.

That night, they made love again, but Alastair did not attempt to put on her restraints. It was as if he had wanted to make his point and that he was now satisfied and had no need to force her submission a second time.

During the next six weeks, Lucinda met Alastair about ten times. She found him an intense lover, always dominating her. Several times, she asked him to tie her up, the experience gave her a strange thrill. At other times, their sessions were calm and free of any trace of tension. Lucinda was sure that she did not love him, yet she was getting more and more emotionally involved with him and got a deeper pleasure from his sophisticated, if unorthodox, sex than she had felt with any of her previous lovers.

One night, they were sitting in the lounge of Alastair's flat and she was explaining how she had been obliged to invent a fictitious boy friend for the benefit of Sarah.

'After all, I could not be meeting my cousin every time over the past two or three months, could I? The trouble is that she keeps on trying to get me to let her meet him. I don't know how much longer I can keep up the sham.'

'Maybe, it won't be necessary in a little while,' Alastair mused.

'What do you mean? Are you getting rid of me?'

Alastair smiled. 'No, not at all. Quite the reverse, if you are in favour.'

For a minute, Lucinda thought that Alastair was going to propose, but she knew him better than that.

'My business is taking me more and more to Paris. Tell me, Lucinda, how would you like to live there?'

'Don't be silly, Alastair. It's all I can manage to pay the rent in London. Unless I can get a decent job, I am stuck where I am now.'

'Don't you be silly, Lucinda. I would set you up in a flat and pay you a reasonable allowance. I'd be over every week or two to stay with you. What do you think?'

Lucinda considered and then with a knowing smile, answered,

'I'll tell you what I think, Alastair. I think that there is something else that you want from me. Something you haven't told me.'

There was a pause. Alastair took a cigarette and lit it very slowly. He gave Lucinda an appraising look before replying.

'Very well, I'll tell you what I have in mind. Of course, I want you to be my mistress and for us to go on meeting. My offer of a flat and an allowance was perfectly genuine. But, beyond that, I want you to help me. If you were in Paris, you could keep an eye on Yves for me.'

'Yves Richepin, your partner?'

'That's the fellow. With your fluent French, you could learn a lot.'

'Why do you want me to spy on him?'

'I have my suspicions of what Yves is up to. As you know, we are partners, I look after the business in London and Yves deals with everything in Paris. I think that he is swindling me, doing business without telling me and pocketing the profits. Will you help me?'

'I'll have to think about it,' Lucinda replied.

But both of them knew that after a respectable interval for thought, she would accept. The prospect of her own flat in Paris was too tempting to refuse. And it might be amusing to get to know the mysterious Monsieur Richepin.

Part 3

7

Hamblewood,
16th April

My dear Lucinda,

Your parents and I were astounded when we learnt that you are now residing in Paris. It was most inconsiderate of you not to have written earlier and to have left us for months ignorant of your whereabouts.

We judged the circumstances of your departure from Hamblewood extremely distressing but at least we had the consolation that when you were in London you were, or so you led us to believe, earning an honest living.

Now that you are established in Paris, we can no longer cherish that hope and we must assume the worst. You do not indicate how you are maintaining your exalted style of living, but I am sure that your expenses are not being paid from the wages of some Swiss waiter.

I am now a fully qualified barrister. In the light of your career to date, it is conceivable that you may have need at some time in the future of the services of a lawyer.

Yours, more in sorrow than in anger,
Miles.

Lucinda irritably threw aside her brother's letter and looked around her. Certainly, her apartment on the Avenue Mozart was a lot more elegant than her digs in Chelsea with Sarah. The building was a solid, stone mansion of the last century, with delicate, patterned iron balconettes in front of the tall windows. The furniture was new but of traditional design – and very expensive. Lucinda had gone to a lot of trouble to find things which were just right for the flat and

Alastair had shown himself to be generous. She had been in Paris for half a year and, by now, she felt thoroughly at home.

She was waiting for the arrival of Yves Richepin who was taking her to lunch. Alastair had suggested that she might stay in touch with his partner and she had been seeing quite a lot of Yves since they had first met.

Alastair had introduced her as a casual acquaintance and had never intimated to Yves that they were lovers and that he was paying for Lucinda's apartment. By playing cool, Alastair had reckoned, it would be easier for Lucinda to win Yves' confidence.

As Alastair had hoped, shortly after their first encounter, Yves had called Lucinda and suggested that they go to a show together. Lucinda had agreed and their meetings had become more frequent and their friendship warmer.

The bell rang and Lucinda went to the door and let Yves in. He was a thick set, burly man with crisp, curly hair and a swarthy complexion. Indeed, he was so dark that he always had a shadow of a beard, even directly after he had shaved. What had made the strongest impression on Lucinda were his hands – hard, calloused hands with short, stubby fingers and wiry hair on his wrists, the hands of a mechanic or a ship's engineer. But Yves was not and never had been an engineer. Lucinda had only the vaguest idea of how Yves earned his living. He was a business man, he told her, but always managed to steer the conversation on to another subject when Lucinda asked him apparently innocent questions. She knew that he was a Corsican and, from something he had let slip in an unguarded moment, she had gathered that he had, at one time, worked as a croupier in a casino.

Yves bustled into the salon and gave Lucinda an approving look as he kissed her on both cheeks.

'Lucinda, you look ravishing this morning. Are you ready to go?'

'Shan't be a minute.'

Lucinda slipped on a light coat and they took the old-fashioned, rickety lift down to the entrance hall. Yves had parked his car nearby but he had discovered a bistro only a hundred yards or so from the flat so they walked in the spring sunshine along the crowded pavement.

As usual, they chatted about trivial things over the meal – what films were showing, where one could buy the best cheese and what Yves thought about English girls. After they had finished eating, Yves seemed in no hurry to leave.

'Don't you have to get back to your office?' Lucinda asked.

'Things are quiet today: I can take my time.'

'You must have a good business if you can leave it to look after itself.' Lucinda's tone was light but Yves could not be unaware of the question that lurked beneath the words.

'That's the way it goes. Sometimes we are frantic: at other times so slack that there is virtually nothing to do.'

Lucinda waited. She had the feeling that Yves was almost ready to open up but he started talking about the racing at Longchamps and asking if Lucinda would go with him there.

They walked back to Yves' car.

'I want to go shopping. Are you going anywhere near the Avenue Montaigne?'

'Jump in. I can drop you there without going far out of my way.'

As they drove through the traffic, Yves asked,

'How well do you know Alastair Grant?'

He was looking straight ahead, his face devoid of expression and his voice was flat and deliberate.

'Nowhere as well as I know you,' she laughed. 'I happened to meet him once in London because a girl friend of mine worked for him. Why do you ask?'

'No reason. I just wondered.'

Yves appeared to be deep in thought. Lucinda asked him

to let her out at the foot of the Avenue Montaigne at the Place d'Alma. As she was getting out of the car, Yves put his hand on her wrist and said,

'We've met a few times, Lucinda, but I would like to see a lot more of you. A lot more.'

'That would be nice,' she breathed.

In his eyes, she could read the struggle which was taking place in his mind. Could he trust her?

'Tonight. Let me bring you back to my place.'

'Why not? Give me a call later this afternoon.'

Lucinda climbed out of the car and waved as Yves pulled away. I do believe that the fish is going to bite, she mused to herself and then made her way to her favourite boutique.

It was eight that evening when Yves came to collect her. Lucinda had prepared herself for her encounter by investing in a new Christian Dior outfit. She noted that her escort had also found time to go home and change into a smart suit and had done his utmost to subdue his bristling beard with razor and talcum powder. They dined in Montmartre and looked in at a nightclub before Yves headed for home.

Yves lived in a spacious apartment in a rather unlikely part of the city, close to the Gare du Nord. All around were shabby shops and small offices and the streets were choked with traffic during the day. By night, however, there was an almost trance-like calm and behind the unpromising entrance of the building, there was a charming, little garden inside a totally enclosed courtyard, onto which Yves' flat looked.

Once inside, Lucinda looked around her curiously, hoping to get some sort of insight into the character of her host. She was disappointed. The contemporary furniture, the tall, green plants, the lithograph views of Paris on the walls, the plain wall to wall carpeting and the handful of paperback popular fiction on the bookshelfs all suggested either a completely nondescript taste or a deliberate attempt to suppress any trace of Yves' own personality. It was the apartment of Mr Average Frenchman which carefully concealed the inner Monsieur Yves Richepin.

Yves brought her a drink from the stereotype cocktail cabinet and put on a record of a romantic, dreamy song which had been popular a few years before.

Even his seduction of Lucinda was according to the textbook. First, Yves settled down on the sofa beside her. Then, in correct sequence, came the arm around her shoulders, the gentle pressure as he pulled her close to him, the brush of his lips against hers as his hand descended gradually to caress her breast. After the prescribed period of petting which was presumably supposed to excite her, Yves led her towards the bedroom.

Lucinda decided that she was not just going to be a routine fuck. She wanted to break through his composure and startle him into revealing something of his true self. Anyway, what had he to hide that was so important?

The moment that Yves took off his clothes, she ceased being the demure, compliant, young girl and seized the initiative.

'Careful,' cautioned Yves for what she had actually seized were his balls. She pulled, twisted and massaged and then forced the not so masterful male to his knees beside the bed. She had twitched off her dress and pulled her panties down. Standing erect before Yves, she thrust her crotch into his face and commanded him.

'Now, you suck me. And good!'

From the fumbling way he obeyed, Lucinda realized that this was a new experience for Yves. She gripped his shoulders and pressed herself forward. He was gasping, fighting for breath, but she gave him no respite.

'Faster! Harder! Work, damn you!'

His lips and tongue were frantically licking, kissing, sucking, striving to satisfy her. Her thighs gripped Yves' head and she found herself hitting his back harder and harder as she spurred him on to greater efforts. She felt her climax approaching and at the moment of exultation, she opened her legs wider to press even more firmly her soaking, hot vulva on to the face of her victim. Yves felt her throbbing which seemed to set his whole body pulsing passionately. With a little moan, Lucinda relaxed and fell back slowly on to the bed. Yves sank to the floor. The mounting rhythm of the girl's orgasm got to him. His own penis had been straining, as if it could break away from the rest of his body and force its way into her and, when she had come, a thick jet of sperm had spurted over the carpet. Lucinda looked down at the prostrate man and smiled at his discomfort.

'Premature ejaculator, eh?'

Yves groaned and heaved himself up on to the bed. Lucinda had to admit that his powers of recuperation were remarkable. It seemed to be only a few minutes before she could feel his swelling member.

'That's a nice resurrection,' she whispered, as she stroked him. This time, she let Yves penetrate her and they made love, lying side by side. She felt that she had made her point. Yves would be allowed to do whatever she wanted when she was ready. There was something of the brute about him and she knew that unless she tamed him at the first encounter, he would impose his will on her and she would never be able to achieve her freedom. But, having forced him to do what she wished, she had achieved a dominance which he would never be able to reverse and his subjection would grow ever more complete.

After that evening, Lucinda saw a lot more of Yves. In addition to their lunches together, she spent many of her evenings with him - in night clubs, at the cinema or at live shows and at his flat. She had jolted the formerly cocksure Frenchman out of his complacency. He did not quite know how to take Lucinda and she was aware of his uncertainty and she exploited it. Sometimes she would be docile, sweet and amenable and Yves would respond with a tendency to being the great macho male. He even seemed to grow taller on those days. Other times, she would be wilfully difficult and capricious. Nothing Yves could do would please her but, when he was in despair, exasperated beyond measure and on the point of losing his temper and breaking with her, she would suddenly become charming and affectionate, completely enchanting him. In a word, Yves was hooked.

However, during all this time, Lucinda never once broached the subject of what Yves did for a living. Then, one day, after they had lunched together and Yves had, as usual, offered to drop her anywhere in town, Lucinda declined the lift, since she had nothing special to do that afternoon.

'Why don't you come along with me?' Yves asked. 'I only need to pass about half an hour in the office and then I shall be free. We could go along to that gallery in the Avenue Matignon where there is that exhibition which you want to see.'

'That would be lovely. But are you sure that I won't be in the way?'

'No, of course not. You can sit in a corner with a magazine while I see to one or two things.'

The office was not at all what Lucinda had expected. It was situated just off the Place de Stalingrad, near the docks which front the canal. All around were North African eating houses, advertising cheap couscous, and dilapidated bars alternated with little shops which displayed a miserable range of undesirable goods. The street was dirty, old newspapers blew across the pavement in the breeze and the local dogs were busy inspecting the contents of the dustbins which were left outside the doors of each building. A few Moroccans or Algerians were sipping tea or red wine at the zinc counter of a sordid, tiny bar to the accompaniment of some blaring Middle East pop music and the clanging and clinking of a couple of pinball machines.

Next to the bar, there was a doorway through which Yves

led the way. A naked light bulb lit a dusty, uncarpeted staircase.

'Do you work here?' Lucinda's tone was incredulous.

'Don't judge by the outside.' Yves flashed a mocking smile at her as they climbed the stairs. At each landing, there was a corridor off which various doors opened. On the third floor, they walked along the corridor until they reached a door on which a small, metal plate announced 'Entreprises Richegrant'. Lucinda, remembering that Alastair Grant had said that Yves Richepin was his partner had no difficulty in interpreting the name of the business.

Lucinda had to admit that the inner office was a distinct improvement on the entrance. She found herself in a small room which was almost totally occupied by a grey, steel desk and a bank of matching filing cabinets. Behind the desk, sat a young, rather sad faced, pimply girl who greeted Yves with a sigh. There were three telephones on her desk, but they stood silent and the girl was engaged in a battle of wits with a crossword puzzle. As Yves had said, they were not busy that day.

'Anybody called?' Yves asked.

The girl shrugged her shoulders and reluctantly folded up the paper with the crossword puzzle.

'Only that kid from Cannes. She needs money – as usual.'

'All right. You don't need to go into details now.'

Yves smiled at Lucinda and the girl relapsed into a gloomy, wary silence. Yves led the way through a door to a more impressive office which was obviously where he worked. He motioned to Lucinda to take off her coat and sit on a sofa in front of which was a coffee table.

'Excuse me for a few minutes, chérie. I'll just go next door and sort out a few things. Make yourself comfortable: I'll get Babette to bring you a cup of coffee.'

Lucinda picked up a glossy magazine which was lying on the table while Yves went through to the outer office and started talking to the pimply girl, who was presumably

Babette. Lucinda strained her ears to hear what they were saying but she could only catch the occasional word or phrase.

She looked around her but there was nothing in Yves' office which would give her any clue as to the nature of his business. There were no trade directories or reference books. The nearest thing to literary works on display was a set of telephone directories. There were no papers of any sort on the desk. The calender was by courtesy of Michelin, the furniture from the Galeries Lafayette, the sculpted glass bowl, the only artistic and costly item in the room, was by Lalique. There was the same anonymity about Yves' office as that which hung over his apartment.

The door opened and Yves came in, carrying a cup of coffee which he handed to Lucinda. He was still talking to Babette through the open door.

'—well, get a few thousand francs down to Cannes then and tell her to settle her bill at the hotel and get packed. Raoul can call round and collect the silly bitch. You know there's an opening coming up in Algiers. We can slot her in there. They don't need brains and she should fill the bill perfectly. But I want a couple of replacements in Cannes. You know who we can use.'

He glanced at Lucinda self-consciously, scribbled some names on a piece of paper and handed it to Babette who had followed him into the room.

'Here you are. Get on with it,' he snapped.

Babette emitted one more sigh and went back to her desk. Lucinda could hear her getting busy on the phone.

'Is everything OK?' she asked Yves.

'Nothing to worry us,' he grinned. 'There's simply a straightforward shipping order to deal with.'

'And what are you shipping?'

'Meat. On the hoof.' His tone was dry and humorous, but Lucinda was not sure that she liked that brand of humour.

Babette wandered back into the room, carrying a letter.

101

'You had better sign this,' she moaned, 'And about those two names you gave me, this one can't make it.' She pointed to the scrap of paper which Yves had given her. 'So, I contacted our latest import from Denmark.'

'Good,' Yves joined in the conspiratorial conversation, 'And what reason did our Number One choice give?'

'Medical.'

'They always pull that one. Get Marcel to check it out and let me know what he says tomorrow.'

The melancholy Babette withdrew and went about her business. There were a couple more similar interludes before Yves announced that he had finished for the day and they were ready to leave.

Lucinda made no comment on what went on in the office. She still did not know the exact nature of Yves' business, but she had formed a shrewd idea of what it might be.

It was some three weeks later that Yves invited Lucinda to spend a weekend in Burgundy. There was to be one of the periodical dinners of the Chevaliers des Tastevins, an organization whose main purpose, it appeared to Lucinda, was to consume as much good food and to absorb as much fine Burgundy wine, as the human frame could withstand. The headquarters of the Chevaliers, the Cos de Vougeot, was one of the most picturesque, mediaeval buildings in France as well as being the home of one of the most celebrated vintages.

All around the majestic mass of the stone mansion with its ancient, wooden wine press and casks which had been in place for centuries, the rolling hillsides were lined with rows of thriving, green vines, rooted in the thin, gravelly soil. The Chevaliers themselves were in ceremonial robes which, together with the setting, gave the whole festivity an aura of dignity. Yves, Lucinda and the hundred other guests all wore formal evening dress.

The eating and drinking and the inevitable speeches went on the whole evening. The seven course meal was preceded by champagne on the terrace and each course was accompanied by several glasses of a different wine from the area and the proceedings were completed by their being served glasses of Marc de Bourgogne, a highly potent brandy made from pressed grape skins. They emerged into the moonlight with the brazen farewell fanfares from the traditional hunting horns, played by musicians in XV Century green costumes, ringing in their ears.

Yves was not drunk but he was more relaxed than Lucinda had ever seen him. Very carefully and deliberately, he steered the car along the narrow roads to Macon where he had reserved a room in a quiet, comfortable hotel.

It was after one when they walked into the lobby of the hotel. As Yves took the key, he was handed a note.

'This telephone message came for you, monsieur,' said the sleepy receptionist.

Yves read the paper with a frown of annoyance.

'Trouble?' Lucinda enquired.

'It's from Babette. I have to call London.'

'What at this time? Won't it wait until the morning?'

Yves shook his head.

'It may be important. The message says to call at whatever hour I got back.'

Upstairs, Lucinda started to remove her make-up, as Yves dialled a number. The conversation was short but stormy.

'For God's sake, it's taken care of, Alastair. No, dammit, I got the bloody girl off to Algiers. That idiot, she would have been useless further east. No, no, no, no! You must leave that sort of decision to me. I know that she would not have lasted five minutes in Beirut or in Cairo. No, Alastair, not even in Istanbul. Believe me, you have no cause for alarm: everything is under control, so go back to sleep. I'll call you again on Monday – or sooner if anything happens but, I tell you, nothing will go wrong over the weekend. You can relax.'

He hung up with a grimace.

'That damned man, why can't he leave us in peace? God knows, I've been running this business long enough. I don't need him poking his nose in to things that don't concern him.'

'So, what goes on in Algiers?' Lucinda asked.

'Nothing, nothing at all. We sent a girl out there for an engagement.'

Lucinda took a deep breath and turned to face Yves.

'You're always very secretive about what you do. But, I'm not that stupid, you know, Yves, my dear. It's white slave traffic, isn't it?'

Yves stared at her. His rage subsided and his tone become more guarded, even apologetic.

'No, Lucinda, chérie, it's nothing like that.'

'Well, what do you call shipping girls overseas? Don't tell me that you are providing nannies to missionaries in places like Beirut or Algiers.'

Yves was silent for a moment. Then he said, very quietly,

'I will be honest with you, since I feel that I can trust you. That was Alastair Grant on the phone. He and I run an agency from the office in Paris. To be frank, it's a call girl business. We have a few hundred girls on the books, mostly in Paris. There are a few in the provinces: some stay on the Riviera and there are some in other big cities like Marseilles or Lyons. Now, you know.'

'That's all very well, my dear, but what the hell has that to do with Algiers or Istanbul?'

'Well, we do get some export orders.'

'And that's not white slavery?'

'No, not at all. The girls know exactly what the score is and they go on short term contracts.'

'And when they get back?'

'Some of them stay on our books.'

'Some, but not all.'

'Lucinda, one has to be realistic. Every business has its casualties. Anyway, that's enough business for tonight. Blast Alastair for spoiling a lovely evening.'

'If the business is in Paris and you run the office, what does Alastair do?' Lucinda called from the bathroom.

'He put up most of the money we needed to get started and he is supposed to find talent from the organization which he has in London.'

They lay, silent, in bed. Alastair's call had shattered the mood. Yves knew it and turned out the light. Minutes passed but Yves sensed that Lucinda was still awake. He spoke quietly.

'Tell me, Lucinda, do you mind?'

'Do I mind what?'

'The business that I am in. Does it make any difference to us?'

'Why should it?'

'Oh, I don't know. The English are not as broad-minded as we are.'

'Maybe I am not a typical English girl. Anyway, Yves, don't worry. I'm not in the least upset. In fact, if I had the opportunity, I would do the same thing myself, provided the money was good.'

'Oh, it pays well enough, I assure you. Perhaps more than you think: even more than Alastair thinks.'

Lucinda tensed with excitement.

'But, Yves, I don't understand. If Alastair is your partner, he must know exactly how much the business pays.'

There was a long pause. Then Yves chuckled and said, 'Well, you see, Lucinda, I keep the books. I am the only one who knows really how much we get from each girl.'

'And that's not the figure which you report to Alastair?' Lucinda asked.

'He gets more than he deserves and he is satisfied, so why spoil him, eh, chérie?'

Lucinda smiled in triumph. Alastair had been right. Yves was stealing from the firm and in their line of business, the Englishman could hardly send in a team of accountants to check the books.

'Yves, darling, I am very tired. I think that I drank enough wine tonight to float a battleship. I'm sorry that Alastair has put you in a bad mood. Let's forget about him and go to sleep. Maybe, it will be better in the morning.'

It was. They made love in that drowsy, half awake state, when every nerve is relaxed and their eyes were still heavy with sleep. Yves took Lucinda with long, unhurried strokes. She found it calm and soothing and it was only as they approached orgasm that their growing excitement dispelled the lingering traces of slumber. Lucinda's senses quickened as she felt Yves' body growing tense until he clutched her convulsively, as he emptied himself deep inside her. Then came the golden afterglow as they lay, side by side, drinking in the warm, bright sunshine which cascaded through the open window. Alastair was forgotten.

They spent the Sunday driving through the mellow countryside and the prosperous, little wine towns of the Côte d'Or. It was an idyllic day and Yves, absolutely at his ease, talked to Lucinda about his family and his childhood in Corsica.

They were poor, country folk and the elder Monsieur Richepin had been a cobbler in a remote village. His brother had been a fisherman and, after the World War, the two of them had gone into the smuggling business. Everything was in short supply in France, and they had found a ready market for American cigarettes, nylons and Scotch whisky which they got from US Army bases. By the time young Yves should have been going to school, he was already a junior member of a network which had its fingers in every sort of racket. The pickings were richer on the mainland, so Yves settled in Marseilles, where he helped in the disposal of the smuggled goods. On the waterfront, life was violent. The Corsicans tended to use knives to get rid of business associates who argued and some of them were hired for political assassinations and even, on occasions, by youthful terrorists whose zeal outstripped their expertise. Yves found gambling and prostitution paid better than the old-fashioned smuggling: he never got into any of the heavier dope rings. It was at this time that he became a croupier and while he was working with a rigged wheel, he came across Alastair Grant. They got talking and Alastair asked Yves if he could find him a woman. Nothing could have been easier. Yves boasted of his connections and of his more lurid underworld adventures. Alastair, for his part, told him that he had put together a number of businesses. He knew his way around and could organize anything. Like Yves, he had a shady past and he had tended to operate in that no-man's land between the legal and the illegal. In an eventful career, he had got to know a number of influential and rich people in a lot of places. So it was that Alastair suggested that they would make a splendid team and that they should go into business together. Yves had agreed and for a while everything went smoothly and they had built up a flourishing business. Alastair had introduced some girls and Yves had no difficulty in finding them employment. But lately, things had definitely deteriorated and Yves was far from satisfied.

'But doesn't Alastair come up with new girls?' Lucinda asked.

They were seated in an old coaching inn at Avallon, on their way back to Paris. It was a romantic spot, steeped in history. Napoleon had stopped there to eat on his way back to Paris after his escape from Elba and the place had hardly changed since those days before Waterloo.

'He's sent over a few, but in the past six months or so, there's hardly been one decent looking kid. I'm the one who does all the work, finding the girls, getting clients, making sure that we have good records and keeping the operation out of harm's way, bribing the odd cop or local councillor, sweetening a mayor, giving a girl as a present to a business man or a reporter who might come in useful. Alastair, the

107

lazy bastard, sits on his arse in London and invests our profits through some Swiss bank he knows. I suspect that he takes a cut for himself there and swindles me.'

'So, you get your own back nearer home,' Lucinda commented.

Yves grinned like a mischievous schoolboy.

They dined at the inn and when the worst of the traffic had driven, nose to tail, back to Paris, they set out for home.

In the car, Yves was, once more, reticent and appeared to be preoccupied.

'What's on your mind?' Lucinda demanded.

Yves gazed at her thoughtfully.

'You know, Lucinda, you are a very pretty girl and you are also very intelligent. That's unusual. What's more, you don't have any stupid prejudices. I bet that you could find some really good material for my business. What I am trying to say is that I think that you would be an ideal partner for me. What do you say?'

'I say that you have already admitted that you steal from your partners.'

'Don't be silly, Lucinda, it would be different with you. We would be working together and I know that I can trust you. You become my talent scout and I guarantee you that you will have it rich.'

'I don't want to get into any trouble with your French police, thank you, Yves. And tell me something else. I've been back to your place several times. If there is so much money to be made, why don't you live in a more luxurious apartment in a fashionable neighbourhood?'

'What, and draw attention to myself! If I moved into the Avenue Foch, I'd have all the flics in Paris after me. To say nothing of every pimp and every informer – and Alastair. No, you come in with me and one day, we'll take a trip to the place I have in the country – not in my own name of course. You'll be pleasantly surprised.'

Lucinda looked at him. She had never seen Yves with

108

such an eager glint in his eye. He beamed at her.

'Well, what about it?'

'It sounds interesting,' she admitted. 'But, I'd like a day or two to think it over. After all, it's a big decision.'

'OK. But don't keep me waiting too long. I want to get this operation really moving.'

8

Next morning, Lucinda was sleepily dunking her croissant in her coffee. The newspaper was propped up in front of her and her gaze passed from one boring story to the next.

But, although Lucinda's body was in repose, her brain was working overtime. Alastair had wanted her to find out for sure whether Yves was swindling him. She had succeeded. For months, Lucinda had enjoyed having her own apartment and being able to buy, within reason, whatever she wanted since Alastair had paid all the bills while he waited for results. Now, if she told him what she had learnt from Yves, and she was sure that she could obtain detailed information on the pretext of considering Yves' proposition that she go in with him, would Alastair continue to foot the bill? She was still Alastair's mistress and he came over to Paris frequently to spend a few days with her, but she had no illusions about their relationship. She enjoyed sex with Alastair and he seemed to appreciate her but she was not in love with him and he was not in love with her. Once she had fulfilled her mission, the cool, calculating Alastair might well dispense with her services and come to a cheaper arrangement with some other girl. After all, in his line of business, there should be no shortage of suitable candidates. There did not seem to be any point in hurrying to provide Alastair with the information he wanted.

On the other hand, to commit herself to a deal with Yves

might prove unwise. Sooner or later, Alastair would become aware of her defection and Lucinda had the impression that he could be a dangerous man to cross. But to turn Yves down would deprive her of a source of income which could replace Alastair's generosity, and it might not be so easy to achieve in practice without setting Yves against her. The longer she could postpone a decision with Yves, as with Alastair, the happier she would be.

Lucinda was in this mood of determined indecision, when a news item in the paper captured her attention. There was a picture of Merton, looking more handsome and more distinguished than ever. She read that he was in Paris for the French première of his latest film. There was the usual scrap of newspaper gossip and the reporter mentioned that Merton was staying at the Hotel Meurice.

On an impulse, Lucinda picked up the phone and called the Meurice. It would be fun to see Merton again. She wondered whether California had changed him. She doubted it: he was too impeccably British to be influenced by the plastic and tinsel world of Hollywood. To her surprise, she was put straight through to Merton by the switchboard without any fuss.

'Lucinda!' His voice was as rich and musical as she remembered. 'How marvellous to hear from you! Are you in Paris for long: can we meet?'

She explained that she was living in the city and was about to accept his invitation, when a thought struck her.

'Is Jennifer with you?'

There was a pause before Merton answered,

'No, it will just be the two of us. I've missed you, my lovely Lucinda: I'm so sated with American womankind. Of course, I invite you to the première, but come and see me this afternoon. Officially, I shall be resting before the evening ordeal. It's Room 553, come straight up. Can you be here about four? Then we can have a few hours to ourselves, undisturbed.'

Lucinda was in a jaunty mood when she entered the lobby of the hotel and took the lift to the fifth floor. She tapped on the massive door and immediately, Merton himself opened it, took her in his arms and kissed her passionately. She followed him into the room and found herself face to face with Jennifer.

Lucinda recoiled but, before she could say anything, Merton took her by the hand and led her across to his daughter.

'I lied to you when you asked whether Jenny was here because I knew you would not have come otherwise. And I cannot stand by while the two women I love are enemies.'

'Please, Lucinda,' Jennifer's eyes were entreating, 'I know it was horrible what I did to you at Cambridge. I caused you and that poor tutor so much trouble. God knows, not one day has gone by without my having regretted my stupid spite. But, you see, Lucinda, I was jealous. I wanted you, I needed you and there was that damned young man taking up all your time and your affection. I felt so excluded. I had to get rid of him. That was all that mattered. I did it because I wanted to have you to myself but all that happened was that I lost you. And now, you hate me. Do you hate me, Lucinda, or can you forgive me? Can we ever be loving friends, like we used to be?'

'Please, Lucinda, for my sake,' Merton's emotion was real and heartfelt, without any of the gimmicks of the stage.

Lucinda looked from one to the other. Her feelings for Michael had long ago receded and left behind merely a sentimental memory, while she had no pangs for having not been able to pursue her university career. Since that day of anger and of shame, life had treated her well and her bitterness had gradually faded into indifference. She recalled the sweetness of her love for Jennifer when they were just schoolgirls and she could not hold back the deep feeling which swelled up inside her. With a sob, she threw herself into Jennifer's arms and the two girls embraced like two long separated lovers.

111

Then, all three of them were laughing, crying and cuddling each other. It was Merton who took Lucinda's arm and steered her towards the bedroom.

'Let's celebrate,' he proposed.

'What, and leave poor Jennifer sitting in the salon, alone?'

'Don't worry about me. I'm coming too.' And Jennifer took her other arm.

It was an unforgettable experience. Father and daughter laid her on the bed and she felt the gentle pressure of their four hands all over her body. Her clothes seemed to slip off and she tingled at the feel of Merton's firm, bare flesh and Jennifer's soft, yielding skin.

She gasped as Merton slid between her legs and she thrilled to his firm, strong strokes, as he held her legs high upon his shoulders. She could not see him, however, since Jennifer had shed her panties and placed her moist, musky scented crotch over her mouth. Lucinda opened her lips and greedily fed on Jennifer's juicy genitals. Jennifer was firmly gripping her arms while her legs were securely in the grasp of Merton. She could not stir, simply receive them both. It was like her taste of bondage which she had both suffered and enjoyed at the hands of Alastair.

It was too intense to last for long. When Merton came, driving deep inside her, she found her whole body to be shaking and pulsing uncontrollably and the excitement was passed on to Jennifer whose thighs tightened against her cheeks. She could hardly breathe, and her face, like her legs, was soaking wet. Then, it was all over and the three of them were lying, exhausted, eyes closed, panting for breath.

Much later, they showered, dressed and set out for the première. Merton was engulfed by a flood of newsmen and women, critics, writers, actors and the inevitable mob of first-nighters. Member of Paris high society and leaders of the fashionable artistic circles monopolized the attention of the great actor, pushing the two girls into the background.

There was a reception after the première but Lucinda

decided to stay only for a short while before going home.

'How long is Merton staying in France?' Lucinda asked Jennifer.

'Poor dear, he's so busy. He has to get back tomorrow evening.'

'Come by my place for drinks in the afternoon before you leave. It's in the Avenue Mozart and easy to find.'

She scribbled down directions, kissed her friend and waved goodbye to Merton. He was sandwiched between a busty woman critic and a very earnest cultural attaché from the British embassy and he rolled his eyes helplessly at her.

She was awakened in the morning by the telephone. It was Yves.

'Lucinda, what happened to you? All day yesterday, I kept calling you but there was never any answer.'

'No, some old friends from England turned up and I spent the day with them.'

'Not Alastair?' There was suspicion in his voice.

'No, of course not, don't be absurd. As a matter of fact, they are coming here for a drink this afternoon at about five? Why don't you drop in and meet them? You can check up for yourself since you obviously don't trust me.'

'Lucinda, chérie, that's not fair. You know I trust you. It's just that I am a rather nervous sort of person.'

'So I have noticed,' Lucinda replied tartly. 'Well, if I don't see you this afternoon, call me this evening.'

It was shortly before five the following afternoon when Merton and Jennifer arrived at Lucinda's apartment. Although they had planned to stay in France only for a couple of days, they seemed to have enough baggage for a Polar expedition, most of it Merton's. They stacked their cases, virtually blocking Lucinda's entrance hall, before settling down.

'We shan't be able to stay for more than a few minutes, darling,' Merton told her, 'But we couldn't leave without coming to see you one more time.'

Lucinda kissed them both, her lovers, father and daughter.

'Have you time for tea or coffee?' she asked.

'Just a drop of Scotch to toast you before we rush away,' Merton answered.

'I'll have a vodka–martini,' Jennifer smiled.

Merton and Jennifer were sitting, chatting with her when Yves arrived. Lucinda led him in and introduced him.

'There you are,' she smiled, 'exactly as I told you, friends from England and not a trace of Alastair Grant.'

Yves looked uncomfortable but he soon lapsed into a subdued conversation with Jennifer while Merton regaled Lucinda with stories of his exploits in Hollywood.

The time passed quickly and Merton had to go for his plane. Yves leaped to his feet.

'I have a car outside. Please, let me drive you to the airport. You wouldn't find it easy to get a taxi at this time of the day.'

'You're very kind,' Merton replied. 'I have to be back in London, so I must not miss the plane. Jennifer is a free agent: she can come and go as she pleases but we poor, old hacks who strut on to the stage have to be at the beck and call of our public.'

'Stop playing to the gallery,' Jennifer told him. 'You'll get no sympathy from anybody if you go on hamming like that.'

They kissed Lucinda goodbye and hurried out to where Yves had parked his car.

'Do keep in touch. I don't want to lose you both again,' Lucinda called to them.

She returned to her unsolved problem of how to stall both Alastair and Yves. It was Yves who worried her, since he was waiting for a definite answer and, as Lucinda had discovered, he was not the most patient of men.

It turned out to be surprisingly easy. When Yves called her, she was on the point of asking for a few more days to think over his proposition but Yves said, 'I'm going to be out of town for a couple of weeks. I'll call whenever I can, but I shall be busy and I cannot tell you in advance when I shall be able to spare the time to phone you.'

'Something to do with your business?'

'Yes, you could say that I am going on a recruiting drive. There are a number of leads which I want to follow up and some of them look too promising to wait. You'll be all right while I am away?'

'Of course. Good luck, Yves. Let me know how you get on.'

During Yves' absence, Lucinda heard little from him. When he did phone, he always was in a hurry or with people, so nothing serious was discussed. However, Alastair did call a couple of times and asked what progress she had made. Lucinda was suitably vague and promised to give him more precise information when he next came to Paris.

Late one afternoon, she was just coming back into her apartment from visiting friends when she heard the phone ringing. Lucinda ran and managed to pick up the receiver before the caller rang off. It was Yves and he sounded in excellent spirits.

'Lucinda, I've been trying to get hold of you. Listen, chérie, I'm back in Paris and I have a wonderful surprise for you.'

'Lovely! What is it?'

'If I were to tell you, it would no longer be a surprise. But you must come over to my place this evening and see what I have brought back for you.'

When Lucinda arrived, she found Yves exultant and excited. He squeezed her, hugged her and kissed her as if he had been away for years.

'Come inside and look at my new treasure. I tell you that I have found a girl who will make our fortunes. When you see her, you will not need any more time to think over whether you join me or not. You will beg to come into the business. And, what's more, she is madly in love with me. She'll do anything that I tell her. Anything. She is wild. Come, Lucinda, meet my new star.'

And, there, standing in the lounge, her eyes glowing, stood Jennifer.

9

Lucinda was astounded and both Yves and Jennifer laughed at her confusion.

'What the hell has been going on?' she demanded.

'It all started the day Yves drove Daddy and me to the airport from your flat,' Jennifer told her. 'I was in no hurry to get back to England but my celebrated father had some boring TV appearance due. While we were in the car, he said what a pity it was that I was going home after so short a stay and sweet, gallant Yves immediately offered to look after me if I cared to stay on for a while. He explained that he had a business trip planned and suggested that I come along. It was all over the South of France from the Côte d'Azur right across to Toulouse. Lovely country! Well, I was a bit reluctant. Not that I didn't want to go with Yves. As soon as I saw him, I thought that he was dishy, but I was afraid that I would be in the way. After all, he said it was business and, of course, I had no idea what his business was.'

'I bet it didn't take you long to find out,' Lucinda remarked.

Jennifer giggled. 'It came as a surprise but it was terrific fun.'

'She was a great help,' Yves interposed. 'You see, I had put an advertisement in the Paris edition of the *New York Herald Tribune*: you know the sort of thing. "Interesting opportunity for girl with sense of adventure and not afraid of meeting people. Prospect of foreign travel. Apply, Box Number so and so.' I got a lot of replies and I arranged to interview the most promising in hotels in different provincial towns. Helps to cover my tracks if there should be any trouble later, can't be traced back to the company or the Paris office, you understand. With Jennifer acting the part of my secretary, things were a lot easier and there were a few girls who were obviously ripe and ready where she helped with what one might call an informal test-run.'

'Do you remember that Sunday afternoon in Nîmes?' Jennifer asked with a mischievous grin.

'Lisette and, what was the other one called?' Yves replied.

'Melisande.'

'That's right, Melisande. God, they were a sporting couple, weren't they?'

'Why do girls in that specific line of business think that they have to adopt such exotic names?' Lucinda demanded.

'My dear,' Yves protested, 'you are doing our two young friends a grave injustice. No, they are not call girls – well, not yet. They are pupils at a strict convent school.'

'What were they doing with a pair of confirmed sinners like you, then?' Lucinda wanted to know.

'Yves and I had been busy with interviews right the way along the coast,' Jennifer told her. 'After doing the smart spots like Cannes and Nice, we had a lively couple of days in Marseilles.'

'I can imagine,' Lucinda commented.

'Well, we had finished on the Friday and we decided to have a few days rest, so we drove through Provence. It was beautiful and very restful. Anyway, we got into Nîmes on the Sunday morning. You know the place: I think that there are more Roman ruins than modern buildings and the gardens where everybody goes for a walk is an ancient cemetery.'

'Lovely but not lively,' Yves explained.

'It was so hot, like an oven,' continued Jennifer. 'We thought that we would have a leisurely stroll before getting out of the place. Under some tall, dark cypress tress, there was an iron seat.'

'And on the seat, there were Lisette and Melisande,' Yves put in.

'I simply had to talk to them,' Jennifer told Lucinda. 'Both of us were wearing the coolest clothes we could find, skimpy shorts and a loose shirt and there were these two girls, perhaps I

117

ought to say, two young ladies, dressed as if they were going to a royal garden party.'

'They even had white gloves,' laughed Yves.

'Laundered linen costumes with skirts below the knees and crisp, starched blouses. I mean, if they had been a couple of old widows, smelling of dried lavender, it would have been understandable, but these were girls in their teens. They looked so odd that I burst out laughing. Well, the kids stared at me: they could not imagine what I found in that city of the dead that was so amusing. So, I asked them, didn't they feel hot in those clothes. One of them, it was Lisette, explained that they were at this very strict school and they had to wear the uniform on Sundays whatever the weather. We got into conversation – they were friendly enough once we had broken the ice and after a while, Yves told them that we were thinking of going down to the river for a swim and asked them if they would like to join us.'

'It would be lovely,' Melisande answered, 'but I am afraid that it would not be possible. You see, we have no costumes.'

'So, let's swim without them,' Jennifer replied.

'The two girls stared at her as if she had spoken to them in Swahili. Then Lisette asked, disbelievingly.

'Swim without clothes, here, in Nîmes? That would not be allowed. It would be a scandal. You know there are a lot of families which come down to the Pont du Gard and picnic under the aquaduct during the weekends.'

'What about if we go further upstream?'

They looked at Yves and then nodded doubtfully.

'Yes, there is a secluded spot that I know,' Lisette told us, 'But it is quite a way from here.'

'Well, we have a car. Come with us. You can show us the way. And wouldn't you like a swim? You can use our towels.'

'Lisette looked at Melisande and Melisande looked at Lisette. Then, with a nervous giggle, Lisette said, 'Why not? Come along, Melisande, it might be fun.'

Yves regarded the two girls and decided that it could, indeed, be fun. Lisette wore her corn coloured hair braided on top of her head like a demure, young maiden but there was a wanton twinkle in her eyes of dreamy blue. Her companion had a fine golden complexion as though she lived all her life in the open air under the golden kiss of the sun. Her auburn hair was pinned up, as was becoming to a prim and proper young lady from a convent school. But Yves' eyes took in the pert breasts of the girls and the shapely swelling of their thighs. Their figures announced that they had barely left adolescence behind and were in the first, radiant flush of womanhood. Yes, it definitely could be fun.

The four of them walked slowly back to where the car was parked. By the time they got there, Jennifer and Yves knew, as well as the names of the girls and where they came from and what their parents did for a living, all about the school where they were virtually imprisoned throughout the week and taught to lead conventional lives by their religious instructors. The prospect of going out with strangers and the audacity of a nude swimming party filled them with anticipation and excitement.

The two French girls were on the point of getting into the back seat of the car when Yves took Lisette by the arm and asked her to sit in front with him and point out the road. Lisette looked nervously at Melisande, but Jennifer called out to her,

'Don't worry. I'll make sure that Melisande is comfortable. You look after Yves,' and she pulled Melisande after her into the back of the car.

'Why don't you take off your jacket: you must be stifling?' Jennifer invited.

'No, not yet, I dare not,' Melisande whispered.

They were driving along a narrow road and, as they approached a dignified, grey stone building, Lisette peered anxiously through the windscreen.

'Down!' she cried.

Immediately both Lisette and Melisande scrambled on to the floor, to the astonishment of the other two.

'What on earth's the matter?' Yves shouted, jamming on the brakes.

'Drive on! Don't stop, please!'

Lisette nudged against his legs and explained, 'You are passing our school. If any of the staff see us in the car of a stranger, we shall be in terrible trouble. We ought to be in church, you know.'

Melisande's head was resting against Jennifer's bare thighs and she enjoyed the sensation of the warmth of the girl's cheek and the faint stirring of her breath against her skin. Casually, she let her hand fall on the carefully groomed hair of her companion and ruffled it affectionately. Imperceptibly, Melisande pressed closer and Jennifer felt her lips, moist against her leg, open and print a tiny, furtive kiss.

'It's OK. You can get up now, we are well clear,' Lisette called, as she got up. But Melisande remained where she was and nuzzled close to Jennifer.

'We are doing fine as we are,' Jennifer told Lisette.

Yves glanced quickly behind him, realized what was going on, and slipped his arm around Lisette's shoulders. She seemed uncertain how to respond to the sudden turn of events but she did not try to remove his hand.

'Wait a minute.'

Jennifer squirmed acrobatically and managed to slide out of her shorts. Melisande impatiently pulled down the flimsy pantees and greedily buried her head between Jennifer's legs, kissing her with the abandon of years of repression being given immediate and undreamed of freedom. Melisande's initiative fascinated the watching Lisette and, after a few minutes, appeared to overcome her own lingering fears and shyness. Diffidently, as if she was frightened that she might be repulsed, she extended her hand and let her fingers play lightly over Yves' rapidly growing erection. He placed his own hand over hers and pushed hard, making sure that Lisette could not withdraw and forcing her to masturbate him firmly. With a little gurgle of delight, she turned towards him, unzipped his shorts and held him tight and lovingly.

'Easy, now,' Yves cautioned, 'Remember that I am driving.

No, don't go away but rub it gently, not too hard and not too fast. At least, not yet.'

However, Yves' enjoyment was short-lived. Lisette climbed back into her seat in order to direct him off the road on to a smaller lane which wound along the bank of the river. Within a couple of hundred yards, they left that road to follow what was little more than a cart track which ended in a clump of beech trees. The trees formed a natural screen around a tiny clearing where the long grass bordered the river bank.

'We can swim here without fear of being disturbed. Nobody ever comes here because the road does not lead anywhere,' Lisette told Yves, as he parked the car beneath the canopy of leaves where the trees afforded welcome cooling shade.

'How clever of you to know this place,' he said.

'Melisande and I found it when we were out on our bikes. We have been here often and we have never once seen another soul.'

As they climbed out of the car and made their way down to where the slow moving water flowed between a few grey, weathered boulders, Jennifer was amused to notice the transformation which had taken place. The crisp, clean, school uniforms were now crumpled and there were sweat stains under the arms of the girls' blouses.

Melisande pulled off her jacket and threw it down on the ground. The grass was warm against their skin as they slipped out of their clothes. Yves tugged Lisette by the arm, but she pushed him away playfully.

'No, everybody must have a turn,' she chuckled. 'Now, I go with Jennifer: you take Melisande – that is if she will have you.'

Yves turned to Melisande, but she dashed down to the bank of the river.

'No, Yves, you will have to wait. You promised that you would take us for a swim, so let's swim.'

'Now wait Melisande, you must finish what you started in the car. Then we can have as long a swim as you like.'

121

Both the girls laughed at Yves. He had torn off his shorts and his swelling penis exhibited for all to see how extreme was his discomfort.

'First we fuck,' he pleaded.

Melisande's answer was to dive into the river. He appealed mutely to Lisette but her eyes mocked him as she followed her friend into the cool water. Yves shook his head sadly. Could this be the same girl who, only a few minutes before had seized him so eagerly while he was driving and could not take full advantage of what she had been doing to him?

'It's no use, Yves,' Jennifer called out to him, 'You will simply have to wait.' She leaped into the river. 'Come on in. It's lovely and the exercise will do you good. It'll take your mind off other things.'

Grumpily, Yves allowed himself to be cajoled into the water. He ducked his head beneath the surface and then struck out vigorously in pursuit of his tormentors.

'Come here, you bloody mermaids! I'll give your damned tails something to remember if I get my hands on you,' he shouted, as he splashed after them.

All four of them were strong swimmers and Melisande had almost reached the opposite bank of the river before Yves caught up with her and grabbed her. They flailed about, shouting and laughing, as the girl pretended to struggle.

'Disgusting! Leave the poor girl alone, you obscene, depraved maniac. If you don't stop molesting her, I shall go and call the police.'

Yves and Melisande stopped their mock fight and gazed up at the far bank in astonishment. There stood a skinny man in his late twenties, shaking his fist at them in fury. His pimply knees poked out beneath the shorts of his scout master's uniform and behind him about half a dozen young boys were watching them, their eyes popping out of their heads with inquisitive excitement. The outraged scoutmaster suddenly realized that all the members of the swimming party were nude and he shooed away his troop of possibly innocent boys.

'Now then, you are supposed to be looking for butterflies and wild flowers,' he shouted at them. 'Get back to the bushes: you won't find anything down here by the river. I can look after these people. Off you go, at once.'

The boy scouts retreated, muttering and tittering among themselves and casting backward glances at the apparition of three naked women.

As the scoutmaster turned his attention back to them, Melisande called out to him,

'It's quite all right, sir. This gentleman is my uncle. He means me no harm: it's just a game.'

'Uncle, indeed! Why are you not wearing bathing costumes like decent people? Such goings-on! Do you want to corrupt my little boys?'

'That could be fun,' Jennifer murmured to Yves under her breath. She and Lisette had come over to join him and Melisande.

'We are naturists,' Melisande called out to him in a tone of sweet reasonableness. 'We all live together in a nudist camp. We believe that the body should be free, especially when it can revel in sunshine.'

'I don't care what you do in your camp,' the scoutmaster retorted, 'but here you can give offence to any passer-by.'

'We thought that nobody was about,' Lisette interposed. 'We do have some clothes on the far bank.'

'It really ought not be allowed,' complained the defender of public decency. 'Please stay in the water until I have led my troop out of sight.'

And with a righteous toss of his head, he set about assembling the boy scouts who had crept back towards the water edge and were peeping surreptitiously at the forbidden fruit which was almost displayed before their straining eyes.

By the time the four of them had swum across to where

they had left their things, the scout troop had withdrawn and they had the place to themselves once more. Jennifer was mightily amused: she said to Melisande,

'You are an accomplished young liar, aren't you? And what imagination! I congratulate you.'

'Well I don't,' Yves grumbled. 'This has put me right off. And it is your fault. I said that we should have gone for our swim afterwards.'

'Oh, you poor thing,' Lisette teased, as she ran her fingers lightly over his balls and dejected cock. 'Have you lost interest in us?'

'I'm not in the mood any more,' Yves told her.

'Let's see if we can put you back in the mood,' Jennifer smiled, as she took a towel and proceeded to rub down Melisande.

'Nobody is going to force you,' Lisette told Yves and she too, turned her attention to her friend.

Yves watched, fascinated. Melisande lay on her back, her eyes half closed against the sun. Jennifer crouched by her head and rubbed her breasts with long, slow strokes while Lisette gently caressed her thighs. With a gentle sigh, Melisande parted her legs and Lisette gently massaged between them, slowly edging her way up until she reached the girl's clitoris. Then, she abandoned her towel and rubbed it deftly with her thumb and forefinger. Melisande seemed to purr with pleasure and the other girls patted and stroked her. Turning on to her side, she spread her legs wide, and Yves found himself staring at the enticing smile of her juicy, red cunt. There was a trace of white wetness, oozing out of her, as though something was frothing and foaming, deep inside her womb. What he saw inflamed Yves: desire, which had been smouldering and which, he had thought had been extinguished, roared into an incandescent flame. Without a word, he pushed Lisette aside and replaced her soothing hand with his insistent, bursting cock.

Melisande gasped as she felt the man upon her and then,

124

inside her; he was pressing down, filling her soft yielding warmth with his masculinity, masterful, potent, menacing. She was unaccustomed to his bigness and she moaned with a pain which was inextricably bound up with the most exquisite pleasure she had ever experienced.

Meanwhile, Lisette had fallen back but her eyes were still fixed on Melisande and her lover. She was surprised by Jennifer, who pushed her on to her back. Her touch was gentle, but it was determined: Jennifer would not be denied and she lowered her own crotch, sweet and fragrant after her bathe, on to the unresisting lips of the young girl. Lisette stretched up her arms to embrace Jennifer's tensed calves as she thrust her tongue deep inside her and sucked greedily, but gently.

'No, you lick my clit,' Jennifer breathed, and she guided the hot, feverish lips in such a way as to give her that glorious, satisfying sensation.

Both of the young girls seemed to have only one object – to give themselves up fully and unreservedly so as to provide Yves and Jennifer with every ounce of pleasure. Yves drove ever deeper and faster inside Melisande while Jennifer exacted total obedience from Lisette. She could feel her orgasm approaching as a strange numbness seemed to be spreading from inside her. Her limbs were threshing uncontrollably and she grasped Lisette's head between her legs so hard and so tight that she could hardly breathe. But Lisette knew that no matter how vice like the grip, she must not relax for an instant: she had to go on serving that throbbing, swollen centre of joy, the very heart of Jennifer's sexuality. There was an explosive moment as Jennifer came and then her body relaxed and she pushed herself off Lisette's recumbent body.

A moment later, there was a cry from Yves and Melisande. Yves' back was arched as he penetrated her right to the hilt and she strained upwards to accept gratefully the hot, white sperm which gushed into her. Yves trembled and then sank limply on to her. Melisande could feel his cock, shrinking within her.

'Please, Yves, don't go,' she implored.

But he laughed and pulled himself free.

'I've come,' he told her callously, 'And so has Jennifer by the look of her. But Lisette is ready. Go on, you two, finish each other off.'

Both girls, wildly excited but still unfulfilled, were in a state where they did whatever they were told and Yves and Jennifer watched them as they took up a sixty nine position and sucked and licked and nuzzled and kissed each other until both of them were caught up in wild paroxysms.

'Feel how wet your face is,' Jennifer whispered in Melisande's ear. The taste of Jennifer and now of Lisette was enough to take her over the brink of excitement. She came, thrusting wildly down on Lisette at the very instant that Yves pressed his hand against Lisette's arse and inserted a finger. Lisette, assailed on all sides, screamed in pleasure as she burst into an orgasm which shook her whole body and left her gasping for breath.

Jennifer and Yves looked down at the sweat soaked, exhausted girls.

'I told you that we should have gone swimming afterwards,' Yves told them complacently. 'Now, look at the state that you are in. We had better have another dip before we leave.'

'So, that was the way we passed our time,' Jennifer told Lucinda. 'What with the swimming and the fucking, I am afraid that we made the two little girls late for afternoon devotions back at their school. And you can see how well Yves trained me in what we might call the more personal aspects of his business.'

'That was quick work, Yves. I congratulate you. But, Jennifer, what did Merton say when you considered going off with a man whom you had met only an hour before and about whom, you knew absolutely nothing? Wasn't he a bit worried?'

'Good God, no, Lucinda. He was too nervous about his TV show to give a damn. Actually, I think that he was pleased to have me off his hands. Remember, I am old enough to take care of myself and Daddy has never played the role of the protective parent. I wrote and told him that I was having a great time and he was as happy as a sand-boy.'

'So, now you are the star turn of Yves' rather special business. You don't mind?'

'Not at all. Yves treats me so well and I adore everything we do together. Pulling girls for him is a sort of challenge and even screwing somebody else to please him turns me on. I bet that you have had some great times with him, Lucinda.'

'And that does not make you jealous?'

'No. Funny isn't it when you remember what I was like over that silly, little Michael. There's something about Yves which gets to me and I can handle absolutely anything with him or for him. The kinkier the better.'

Yves wanted the three of them to spend the night together, but Lucinda was not in the mood and she made some excuse to leave after they had dined. Jennifer's arrival on the scene had been something of a shock and she was not yet sure whether she was pleased with this development or not. It might turn out to be an unwelcome complication in a situation which already threatened to get out of control.

With a sigh of relief, she let herself into her flat and immediately tensed. There was somebody there. Whoever it was was not making any effort to conceal his presence. The reading lamp was on in the lounge and the radio was playing. Lucinda walked into the lounge and, sitting in an armchair, was Alastair.

'Welcome home,' he purred. 'I got here some time ago. Have you been out with Yves?'

'No, I was with a girl friend. Sorry that you have been waiting. If you had let me know that you were coming, I'd have been here to greet you.'

Why had she lied? Lucinda was not sure but she felt that she was not ready to denounce Yves to Alastair. Indeed, she had not yet made up her mind whether to betray Yves or keep silent. It would be better if Alastair did not know how intimate she had become with Yves. Not yet anyway.

Alastair gave her a long, penetrating stare, but said nothing more about his Corsican partner.

'It's a bit late. Where shall we go for dinner?'

'Sorry, darling, but I've already eaten. Let me fix you something from the kitchen.'

She brought him some cold meat, cheese and a bottle of wine. During the meal, Alastair asked what she had been doing and Lucinda was suitably vague. When they went to bed, Alastair said that he was tired and they went to sleep without making love. This did not worry Lucinda: Alastair was an unpredictable performer between the sheets. Some nights, he was violent and almost insatiable but there had been others when he was completely indifferent to the very idea of sex.

Lucinda wondered how she would cope when Yves phoned. Luckily, he never arrived unexpectely, so she did not fear him bursting in and discovering her with Alastair.

They were sitting at breakfast when the phone rang. Lucinda steeled herself, but it turned out to be Jennifer. They chatted for a few minutes and arranged to meet later that day.

'Was that the girl you were with when I got here yesterday?' Alastair asked.

'Yes, she's an old school chum over from England.'

Alastair nodded. He seemed satisfied and Lucinda was pleased, as though she had been able to authenticate her story.

Alastair wanted to visit Yves at the office, but first he checked into a hotel so as to keep Yves ignorant of his relationship with Lucinda. She spent the following day with Jennifer who told her all about her exploits with Yves on his 'recruiting drive'. Lucinda marvelled at how completely

128

Jennifer was captivated by Yves and how rapidly she had fallen under his spell. As Yves had told her, Jennifer was ready to do anything and she had already completed an impressive list of what, in mock-scientific jargon, she termed 'sexperiments'.

That evening, Lucinda was faced with a delicate turn of events. Jennifer was staying at Yves' apartment and Lucinda had taken her back there, after going to a movie. Lucinda knew that Yves would still be in the office, presumably with Alastair, so she had no qualms about going into the empty flat with her friend. While they were sitting there, the phone rang.

Jennifer picked it up. It was Yves and he wanted Jennifer to meet him for dinner. She repeated the name of the restaurant and the time of their rendezvous. She was about to hang up, when she added,

'Oh, by the way, Yves, darling, Lucinda is here with me. Do you want to talk to her?'

Lucinda cursed silently, as she took the phone. Yves pressed her to come along with Jennifer. If, as was likely, Alastair was in the room with Yves, the damage had been done. He would know that Yves was on more than friendly terms with her girl friend. It was the sort of thing to arouse the suspicions of a more trusting type than Alastair.

Her worst fears were confirmed when she and Jennifer entered the restaurant for, sitting beside Yves, was Alastair. He made an elaborate pretence that he had not seen Lucinda since the meeting when he had introduced her to Yves. For his part, Yves proudly showed off Jennifer to Alastair and she, in turn, being unaware of Lucinda's predicament, made no secret of her intimacy with Lucinda. Alastair spoke little during the meal, but Yves chattered incessantly while Jennifer looked on dotingly. Beneath the surface, Lucinda felt a tension between her and Alastair. It was a difficult evening.

The meal over, Yves took Jennifer back and dropped

Alastair at his hotel and Lucinda at her flat. Once inside, she called the hotel and was put through to Alastair's room.

'Do you want to come over?' she invited.

'No, I don't feel like going out again tonight. I'm taking an early flight in the morning.'

'I thought that you might want to have a talk with me before you went back,' she suggested lamely.

'I don't think that there is much to talk about. After all, you had all last night to tell me your story. Jennifer was, of course, your girl friend, the one you were with when I got into Paris and when you were not with Yves.'

'That's right. But, Alastair, what I told you was true. I've known Jennifer for years.'

'And, I suppose you introduced her to Yves. I must say that you make a very nice, tight trio. Are you sure that you don't know more about Yves than you have told me? I wouldn't like to think that you were having a little game with me, Lucinda.'

She needed time to sort things out. If only she could allay Alastair's doubts, she would have a few days or weeks in which to arrange something.

'Alastair, you are being hysterical. Look, this girl and her father happened to come to Paris and Yves met them by chance when he passed by my place. I wasn't to know that the silly bitch would fall head over heels in love with him. It's nothing to do with me. In fact, it makes it more difficult for me to get close enough to Yves to find out exactly what he is up to.'

It was not true, but it sounded good enough: she just hoped that it was convincing.

'Very well, Lucinda, if that's the way things are.' Alastair's voice gave nothing away. 'I hope that in a short time you will be able to tell me something more positive. You know where you can get in touch with me. I want to hear from you. And soon, don't wait too long, will you, Lucinda.'

Those were the last words she was ever to hear from Alastair's lips.

10

So, the crisis had passed. Alastair had been safely back in London for more than a week. Her monthly allowance had arrived promptly in her bank and Lucinda felt a wave of relief. Meanwhile, she was under no immediate pressure from Yves who was content to wait for her to come to him. His attitude had changed as a result of his conquest of Jennifer, who was absolutely besotted by him. Yves' apparent indifference was meant to convey to her that, as a talent scout, she was dispensable and, while her presence would be welcome, he and Jennifer could manage quite adequately without her until such time as she came to her senses. Day by day, things drifted on and Lucinda was not obliged to come to any decision as to whether to join Yves or to betray him to Alastair. That state of affairs suited her fine.

The morning that Jennifer came round to her flat, Lucinda's first reaction was that she had been sent by Yves either to spy on her or to try a little gentle persuasion. However, Jennifer insisted that Yves was out of town.

'He had to go and sort out some trouble with a girl in Cannes. He said that he might be away for a day or two. There's this dreadfully miserable kid, Babette, who is running the office while he is not there, so I am at a bit of a loose end. Anyway, I wanted to come and see you, Lucinda. You've no idea how happy I am.'

Jennifer looked radiant, and Lucinda felt a pang of jealousy.

'With Yves?'

'With Yves.'

'You'd better have a cup of coffee. It's good for getting

your nerves under control.'

'Lucinda, don't be bitchy! Please, darling. I am so happy and I want you to be happy, too. And Yves. It's the three of us. You are part of us, you know.'

Lucinda shook her head.

'Not like that. You belong to Yves. I don't.'

'You will. You'll see. He will tame you and you will love it. You know, I worship that man: I'm in heaven when I am with him.'

'Really, Jennifer? It's not very long ago when you were telling me how much you were in love with me.'

'But I do love you, Lucinda. I love you both. Come, my darling, let me show you how much I love you.'

Jennifer took Lucinda by the hand and led her into the bedroom. Lucinda's jealousy gave their lovemaking a new dimension of passion. She wanted to hurt Jennifer at the same time as she exulted in her beauty. Jennifer's response was equally violent. They clutched roughly at each other's bodies, scratching as they caressed and biting as they kissed. Each set about punishing her mate with the savagery of her embrace and they tore at each other like wild animals. In their sexual frenzy, there was not a trace of tenderness, yet there was a great and rare love. A quarter of an hour later, completely absorbed in the possession of each other and oblivious to the rest of the world, they were lying naked, bathed in sweat, their hair bedraggled, their lips swollen with bites and kisses when the police arrived.

When they first heard somebody knocking at the front door, both girls decided to ignore the interruption: they considered that they were engaged in more pressing business. But the knocking continued and, as Lucinda finally jumped out of bed, the door swung open, the flimsy lock was no match for the skill and experience of the Parisian police, and she found herself facing two uniformed men and an inspector in the inevitable raincoat and soft hat – just like the movies, as Lucinda was to recount later.

In fact, Lucinda's recollection of what took place was rather vague and confused. It was all so sudden, so unexpected, such a shock and it happened so fast. The men looked at the nude women with evident contempt and disgust. They refused to answer any questions, simply giving them barely enough time to grab the nearest clothes, before bundling them out of the apartment. They did not bother to wait for the lift, but hurried down the stairs and out into the waiting police car. Lucinda cringed before the stares of the *concierge* and passers-by on the pavement. Their eyes seemed to accuse her and to mock her. She had had no time to arrange her clothes or to fix her make up and she felt as naked and as vulnerable as at the moment when the police had discovered her, practically in the arms of Jennifer.

In the car, she demanded to know if she was being arrested and, if so, for what offence. She was told only that her questions would be answered down at the station. Jennifer hardly spoke: she was sobbing quietly, her face drained of colour and her eyes staring wide with shock.

In the police station, they were separated. Lucinda was pushed into a waiting room – and kept waiting. The only furniture was a plain wooden table and a couple of hard chairs. A single, black telephone stood on the table along with a few sheets of blank paper. The walls were bare and looked as if they had not been painted for decades. She sat there, on one of the chairs, facing the table, waiting in silence. Her mind was in a turmoil and she was shivering with apprehension.

An eternity passed.

Then the door opened and the police inspector came in, escorted by an assistant who carried a fresh notepad and a tape recorder with a cassette.

'You are Mademoiselle Farrer?'

Lucinda nodded.

'Please speak up so that your answer can be recorded.'

'Yes.' Her voice was unnaturally husky.

'And you are living at Number 36, Avenue Mozart in the Sixteenth Arrondissement?'

Unexpectedly, Lucinda's anger overcame her fear.

'Tell me, why am I here?'

'Please answer my question, mademoiselle.'

'Why the hell should I answer your question? First, you tell me why I have been arrested.'

'It is not my function to discuss with you the reasons for your being here. I am only interested in confirming your identity. Then you will be seen by an interrogating judge who will be competent to deal with these matters.'

'Where I live, you have to tell anybody you drag into a police station the reason for his arrest and the accused has a right to see a lawyer.'

'Mademoiselle Farrer, I can assure you that you will be dealt with according to French law and justice. Now, will you please confirm your address?'

'Not until you tell me why I am here.'

'It is of no great consequence. We know where we found you and witnesses can be produced who will testify that you have been living there. However, we shall make a note that you have refused to co-operate with the police in a routine enquiry.'

The two policemen got up and left the room. Once more, Lucinda was absolutely alone in the bare, silent room.

Another and even longer eternity passed before the door opened again and a middle-aged man entered, again with an assistant to take notes. He introduced himself as a *juge d'instruction*, an examining magistrate.

'My function is to consider the charges which have been made against you and, after interrogating you, to see whether you have a case to answer. Afterwards, if it becomes necessary to proceed against you, I shall be responsible for the presentation of the case. I do not decide whether you are innocent or guilty. Is that clear?'

'Please, will you tell me what I am accused of?'

He regarded her coldly and his tone was indifferent rather than hostile.

'Certainly, Miss Farrer. Accusations have been made that you are engaged in an unlawful activity, namely you are living off immoral earnings. You understand?'

Lucinda shook her head in puzzlement.

'Come now, Miss Farrer. You are not a child. Must I spell it out for you? What is said, is that you are running a chain of prostitutes and call girls, that is how you earn your living. It is also alleged that you have engaged in acts of gross indecency with a Miss Maxwell, but since you are both adults and such acts were not committed in public, that is not an offence, in the legal sense, so it does not concern me.'

'What about Miss Maxwell? She was brought in with me. Are the same charges being brought against her?'

'At this stage, Miss Farrer, there are no charges, only accusations. I shall decide whether charges will be brought. As for Miss Maxwell, since you are concerned, less serious complaints have been made against her. It is said that she is living as a prostitute and has never been registered.'

The judge's questions were precise and searching. It became clear to Lucinda that a considerable amount of evidence had been brought against her. In a word, she had been framed.

Eventually, she was visited by an official from the British Embassy. She protested to him her innocence, but he seemed unimpressed. After all, what was a young girl doing, living in an expensive flat in Paris without obvious source of income and never receiving money from her family? In despair, Lucinda mentioned the name of Miles and stated that her brother was a prominent member of the Bar. That did make some impression on the impassive official.

She spent the night in a cell and was examined by the judge again the following morning. The dossier of her case was bulky and the sheaf of paper in the hands of her

135

interrogator was like a hidden weapon, aimed at her. Over and over again, she was asked about women she had never met, places she had never visited, payments she had never received. She denied everything, but had no idea of whether her protestations were believed or not.

After her second night in jail, Lucinda was demoralized and in despair. She had slept badly and her head ached. Prison did not agree with the Honourable Lucinda Farrer.

She was brought back into the miserable waiting room, resigned to another session. She noted that when she came into the room, her judge was waiting for her together with two other men.

'Miss Farrer, you do appreciate the gravity of the accusations which have been brought against you?'

Lucinda read disdain and disgust in the eyes of the examining magistrate as he addressed her. She nodded weakly: she felt too defeated to argue or to try to defend herself further.

'Certain representations have been made on your behalf as a result of which, it has been decided not to proceed with the case against you.'

Lucinda was sure that she must have misheard the words. She stared at the men in disbelief.

'Don't you understand? We are going to let you go.'

'I'm free to leave? I don't have to stay here any longer?'

'It was not my decision,' replied the judge severely. 'You have some influential friends, young lady. But you are being released on two conditions.'

Lucinda waited.

'First, you will leave France immediately and you will not return for at least six months while some aspects of this matter are cleared up. If you visit our country subsequently, we expect you to behave yourself. You agree?'

'Yes, of course.'

'The other condition is that you are to be entrusted into the custody and the protection of a gentleman who is waiting next door for you.'

It must be Alastair, Lucinda thought. The whole business reeks of him and now, he has come to claim me.

They led her through to an outer room and handed her over, like an unwanted parcel, to the man who was waiting for her impatiently. Her deliverer was not Alastair. It was her brother, Miles, who led her out of the police station and stayed with her while she gathered up her belongings from the flat. He never left her alone for a minute until they had boarded the plane for London. She quit Paris without being able to contact Yves or to find out what had happened to Jennifer. For the second time, she came home to Hamblewood, in disgrace.

'It took a great deal of influence and quite a bit of gentle bribing to get you off the hook,' Miles informed her. 'Of course, I knew that you would get into trouble, Lucie. It was only a question of time, so I was prepared for the news when it came. But, I warn you, my baby sister, this is the last time that I'm going to do the knight in shining armour stuff. The next time you get into some scrape through your foolishness or your immorality, you are on your own. You are a disgrace to the family. You mother and father are ashamed of you – and so am I.'

Such were the sentiments of Brother Miles.

Lucinda was sure that her ordeal had been engineered by Alastair who must have concluded that there was a conspiracy between her, Jennifer and Yves against him. She did not know what had happened to Jennifer. But, in Alastair's eyes, Jennifer was of no importance, a mere pawn and her problem with the French police was not likely to prove too serious. But, Lucinda wondered, what had Alastair in store for Yves who, he must have considered, to have been the arch villain who had corrupted Lucinda and used Jennifer.

Three weeks later, she found out when she read in the newspaper that the body of Yves Richepin had been washed ashore near the yacht basin at Monte Carlo.

Part 4

11

The days following Lucinda's return to the ancestral home were not happy ones for her. Miles never tired of reminding her that she owed her deliverance to a combination of his growing legal reputation and the family's prestige – and wealth. Her mother remained aloof: it was not dignified for an aristocratic lady to discuss the more sordid aspects of Parisian low life. Her attitude to her daughter was one of resigned acceptance, tinged with distaste. Her father was far too occupied with the business of running the great estate and with the careful perusal of the sporting and financial columns of the newspapers to be concerned with so unimportant a matter as the life of his erring offspring. So, by the members of her family, Lucinda was, in turn, condemned, patronized and ignored.

She was restless. After her taste of freedom in France, she found her old friends and acquaintances dull and provincial. Her attempts to contact the Maxwells were unsuccessful. The hotel where Jennifer had been first registered when she came to Paris with her father had no forwarding address. There was no reply from Yves' flat when she phoned. As for Merton, he had apparently disappeared from the face of the earth. Lucinda eventually learnt from his agent that Merton had been overdoing things and was badly in need of a prolonged rest. Consequently, he had taken off for an undisclosed hide-out with strict instructions that he was not to be disturbed by mail, phone calls, visitors or bills. Despite all her attempts at persuasion, the agent steadfastly refused to help her contact the resting actor, nor would he forward any message.

'If I were to make an exception for you, young lady, he

would never have another moment's peace. Nothing, but nothing, is going to disturb Merton for the next six weeks. I have promised, as the only concession, that if the end of the world is due, I shall give him half an hour's warning. Nothing else gets through.'

Alastair never made any attempt to reach her and Lucinda came to the conclusion that if he had been, indeed, the cause of her arrest, his desire for revenge had been satisfied. But when she read the news of Yves' death, her doubts and her anxiety were renewed. She took the opportunity of a day in London to call on Sarah Brown. Lucinda wanted to phone first, but she had lost Sarah's number and since the flat and the phone were not in her name, there was no way she could find it from a directory. However, it was a Saturday and Lucinda knew that Sarah did not work at the week-ends, so there was a good chance that she would find the Australian girl at home.

'Oh, it's you. And what the hell do you want?'

Sarah's greeting was decidedly on the cold side and it caught Lucinda unprepared. She gazed at the tall, ash blonde girl in astonishment.

'I just wanted to talk to you for a few minutes. I've had a lot of problems and I hoped that you might be able to give me some news of Alastair. Can't I come inside?'

'If you insist.'

Sarah stood aside to let Lucinda into the room which, not so long ago, had been home to her. Now, she felt an unwanted stranger. Sarah stood, waiting for her to speak: she did not even invite Lucinda to sit down.

'What's the matter? Why are you so hostile towards me?' Lucinda asked.

Sarah laughed drily.

'Poor, little Lucinda! You think that the moment that you get into some trouble, you can come creeping around here as if you had never done anything wrong. You've got a fucking cheek, Lucinda. I was the one who got you a temporary job

142

with Alastair and how did you repay me? You went crawling behind my back, meeting him in secret and stealing the prize job of the outfit in Paris. Didn't you ever think for a minute that it should have been me, sitting out there? And it would have been, if you hadn't gone flashing your fanny around.'

'You've got it all wrong,' Lucinda cried. 'It was Alastair who made all the running. He never suggested that he had you in mind for the Paris assignment. You were the reason I got the job. Don't you remember, you introduced me because I spoke good French. When his secretary was away—'

'You don't have to remind me. I'll never forget that it was me who got you the job and what a treacherous, little bitch you turned out to be.'

'Well, you don't speak French, so how the hell do you think that you would have coped?' Lucinda swallowed her anger. 'Look, Sarah, I'm sorry. I never intended to steal your job. But, you can have no idea the trouble I have had. I even got thrown into jail.'

'Yes, I know,' Sarah grinned. 'Alastair told me.'

'So, you know what Alastair did to me?'

'Alastair? What makes you think that Alastair was responsible? The way you were behaving in Paris, it was certain that you would end up in trouble and you only got what you deserved. Alastair didn't get you sent to jail: he was the one who helped to get you released. Not that you wouldn't be improved by a few years where you belong, behind bars.'

'Alastair got me released!' Lucinda yelled. 'Don't be stupid, it was my brother who managed it. And if Alastair was not the guy who had me put away, who was it who blew the whistle on me and told the police a pack of lies?'

'Why it was your friend, Yves, of course.'

'Yves is dead. I read in the paper that his body has been washed up. Are you going to tell me that Alastair had nothing to do with that also? It was just a coincidence that Yves got murdered after I had been arrested and Alastair is sobbing his heart out somewhere in grief for the two of us?'

'So that's what you think! Really, Lucinda, you have a vivid imagination. No, it was Yves who had you picked up by his pals, the cops. You had a sweet, little racket going with him but, greedy slut that you are, you double-crossed him. So, he got his own back on you. Alastair found out about it and he was pulling strings behind the scenes to get you released while your precious brother was making a big public show and not getting anywhere. As for Yves, you must have known that he was a gangster, one of a Corsican mob. A rival gang did him in. Happens all the time in the circles you've got yourself into. So, why don't you take your sweet arse off back into the country and grow roses or raise pigs or whatever it is that your noble Daddy and Mummy do to pass the time.'

Lucinda stared at her. Sarah's explanations had a logic, but when Lucinda recalled Alastair's hints and menaces the last time she spoke to him, she was unconvinced.

'I would like to see Alastair, if what you say is correct. Sarah, I had no deal with Yves. If Alastair thinks that, he is mistaken. And there are things that I ought to discuss with him about the Paris office.'

Again, Sarah laughed bitterly and without a trace of humour.

'Sure, you would like to see him, but I don't think that he would want to see you. And, as for the Paris office, you need not worry about it. Your successor will clear up any problems out there.'

'My successor?'

'That's right innocent, little Lucinda. Your successor. For your information, that's me. I'm off tomorrow to take your place in Paris – even though I don't speak fluent French, like you. But, I don't work against my boss or my friends behind their backs, so perhaps I shall make out better than you did.

Now, if you don't have anything more to say, why don't you walk out through that door and keep on walking?'

There was nothing more to be gained by further discussion. Sarah obviously believed her own version of what had happened.

If Alastair were guiltless, she would rather have heard an account from Alastair himself, but Sarah was not going to help in bringing them together and Lucinda sensed that an unprepared visit to the London office of Alastair might be asking for trouble. So, she left and went home without having achieved anything.

When, a few weeks later, a bronzed, relaxed and rejuvenated Merton returned to London, Lucinda rushed to see him and to tell him what had happened. She hoped that he had some news from Jennifer but she was disappointed. Merton's isolation had been complete and there was no message awaiting him from his daughter.

'But that's a good sign, Lucinda,' he assured her. 'You know that Jenny is an independent girl. I often don't hear anything from her for months on end and then she will turn up without a word of warning. But if she had any trouble, she would have got word to me and there would have been a cry for help waiting for me in London. Don't worry, I am sure that she is OK. She has got out of worst scrapes before now. Don't worry! We shall hear from her soon. Be patient. You see, Jennifer will pop back into your life when you least expect it.'

Lucinda was to find that Merton's prophecy was to prove uncannily accurate.

12

As the days went by, new friends, new lovers, new interests began to take up Lucinda's time, but the unanswered

questions about her relationship with Alastair and her
doubts about the circumstances of Yves' death, were never
far from the surface of her mind. For weeks, she was left in
absolute peace and she heard nothing more of what had
happened, or was, for all she knew, still happening, in
France.

The lull was broken by a phone call from an unknown
man.

'Miss Farrer? My name is Fothergill, Arnold Fothergill
and I am a solicitor. I would like to meet you to discuss some
rather important business. Would you, by any chance, be
planning on coming to London this week?'

'Yes, as a matter of fact, I was thinking of taking the early
morning train on Wednesday. Just what is this business
which you want to discuss?'

'I would rather not talk about it over the phone, Miss
Farrer. Suffice it to say, that it is of considerable urgency
and it is imperative that I see you.'

'Very well. Wednesday afternoon, then. Where is your
office, Mr Fothergill?'

'It would be far better for us to meet outside my office.
From two o'clock onwards, I shall be in suite 1411 at the
Savoy and I shall wait for you there. Don't bother to check
with reception, come straight up.'

'Now, just a minute.' Lucinda protested. 'What sort of an
idiot do you take me for? An unknown man phones, claims
to be a solicitor, won't disclose his business, refuses to see me
at his office and expects me to turn up at a hotel room.
Alone, I presume, Mr Fothergill!'

'Oh, definitely alone, Miss Farrer.' The man did not seem
in the slightest put out by her attempt at sarcasm. 'Yes,
please do not bring anyone with you. However, I do
appreciate that this approach must be sufficiently uncon-
ventional to arouse your suspicions. I do assure you that it is
absolutely genuine. I understand that your brother is a
barrister. You can easily verify with him that there is such a

146

firm as Fothergill, Hardy, McGill and Tweed and that the senior partner is, indeed, Arnold Fothergill. Please, believe me, I am that Arthur Fothergill and I must see you on Wednesday.'

Before she could argue further, the man had hung up.

'Miles, do you know anything about a Mr Arnold Fothergill who claims to be a solicitor?'

Her brother glared at her.

'Now what foolishness are you getting mixed up with?'

'Please, Miles, can't you answer a simple question? Do you happen to know a solicitor called Fothergill?'

'There are thousands of solicitors in London and God knows how many outside. As it happens, I have come across an Arnold Fothergill, but I don't know whether it is the same man as you have in mind. It might be another fellow with the same name.'

'I don't suppose that there can be too many solicitors with that name running around,' Lucinda scoffed. 'Really, Miles, sometimes you take your legal caution to ridiculous extremes.'

'It's a pity that you have not shown something of the same caution in your own conduct, Lucinda.'

She sighed and suppressed an urge to punch her unctuous brother on the nose. With measured restraint, she asked sweetly, keeping her voice as controlled as possible, 'Please, Miles, tell me what you know of the Arnold Fothergill you have met.'

'I never met him, but I have heard something of his reputation. Seems that he is an able lawyer but specializes in rather dubious affairs. Not well thought of by members of the Bar.'

'You mean that he is bent?'

'Lucinda, why are you so crude? It is a very serious matter to make allegations of that nature about a lawyer – you can get into a lot of trouble.'

'Miles, there are just the two of us. I am not holding a

press conference. Now, tell me, in your candid, professional opinion, but without any responsibility on your part, dear brother, is Arnold Fothergill a crooked lawyer?'

'Do I have to answer yes or no?'

'For God's sake, Miles!'

'All right. Yes, I think so, although I have no proof, you understand. I would strongly advise you against getting involved with Mr Arnold Fothergill.'

Miles' solemn warning was all that Lucinda needed to persuade her to keep her mysterious appointment and so, that Wednesday, she made her way to the Savoy and knocked at the door of Suite 1411.

'Come in, Miss Farrer, and sit yourself down.'

Arnold Fothergill was a balding, fifty year old cherub. But above his chubby, rosy cheeks, were keen and calculating blue eyes. He had removed his jacket and Lucinda marvelled at the splendours of his purple braces which clashed stridently with the deep blue and white stripes of his shirt. His voice was deep and his tone as treacly as that of a used car salesman. Lucinda's first reaction was to be on her guard: Arnold Fothergill struck her as a slippery customer.

She refused his offer of tea or a stronger drink.

'Right, let's get down to business, shall we?'

'Yes please, Mr Fothergill. That's why I am here.'

'Very well, Miss Farrer. I represent Mr Alastair Grant, in an unofficial capacity, if you follow me. What we are going to discuss, is a matter of the greatest confidence – a very delicate affair, I do assure you. I am going to take you into our confidence and I expect you, for your part, to be just as forthcoming and open with me.'

'What is this all about, Mr Fothergill?'

'Now, Miss Farrer, you and Mr Grant were lovers. That is so, isn't it?'

Lucinda stared at him.

'I really do not see that is any business of yours, Mr Fothergill.'

'Come, Miss Farrer, I would not bring the matter up if it were not relevant. Of course, you were lovers. After all, you were living in a flat in Paris which was paid for by Mr Grant. That is a fact: you don't deny it, do you?'

'No,' Lucinda replied with measured deliberation, 'Since you seem to know so much about my private life, there would be no point in denying it. I suppose that you know also that I was forced to quit Paris after being framed by your client.'

'Now, Miss Farrer, you are making a big presumption and a big mistake.' Fothergill's voice was serious, but there was something of a twinkle in his eyes. 'Of course, I know about your being arrested. Very embarrassing for you, my dear, and I assure you that Mr Grant was very sympathetic. It was not Alastair Grant who was the cause of your little brush with the police. On the contrary, it was thanks to his contacts that you were released. Now, reflect, Miss Farrer, Mr Grant has done you a number of favours – the flat in the Avenue Mozart, a generous allowance and, at considerable inconvenience and expense, eventually effecting your release from custody when you were in danger of facing a most serious charge in the courts. By any reckoning, you are under a moral obligation to Mr Grant.'

'What are you getting at, Mr Fothergill?'

'To put it bluntly, Mr Grant has done you a few good turns, now, he would like you to reciprocate and do something for him.'

'What does he want?'

'Tell me, Miss Farrer,' Fothergill appeared to go off at a tangent, 'do you keep a diary?'

'Yes.'

'Do you happen to have it with you?'

'Yes.'

'Excellent! Do take it out and consult it.' Arnold Fothergill put on a pair of rimless spectacles and peered at a paper which he took from a brief-case. 'It was on 12 May

149

that you were obliged to leave France under the unfortunate circumstances which we have discussed. That's right, isn't it?'

Lucinda looked at her diary and nodded.

'Now, Miss Farrer, do you have a note of what you did and where you were on the evening of 25 May?'

She turned the pages and then answered.

'Yes. I was in London for the day. I came up for a show and I spent the night at our house in Belgrave Square.'

Fothergill smiled approvingly.

'Forgive the question, but did you spend the night alone in that house?'

'Yes, as a matter of fact I did. The house had been shut up since the family were staying in the country and the servants had been given a short holiday. It was too late after the show for me to get back to Hamblewood and it would have been stupid to stay in a hotel for the night when the house was available.'

'Just so, Miss Farrer. You were very wise.' Fothergill's tone was smoother and more urbane than ever. 'Now, I suggest to you, Miss Farrer, that you might have made an error when you made that entry in your diary and that Mr Grant spent the night with you in Belgrave Square. It just slipped your memory perhaps, or you felt that you did not want to write that in your diary in case it fell into the hands of somebody who might make trouble for you if they read that sort of thing.'

Lucinda stared at the pompous, little lawyer but he returned her gaze unflinchingly.

'No, Mr Fothergill, absolutely not. You know that I suspected Alastair of being responsible for my trouble in France. It's hardly likely that I would sleep with him, is it?'

'But, it was natural that you should be worried by the thought that Mr Grant, who had been your lover, had struck at you by having you arrested. You must have been terribly upset and so you phoned him to have it out with him. Mr Grant told you that he had not been responsible for your problem. That was when you invited him to come round to the house and explain what had really happened. When he arrived, he informed you that you had been the victim of the malice of Yves Richepin. You were reconciled. I don't doubt that tears flowed, there was great tenderness and, in a wave of loving emotion, you found each other again between the sheets.'

'Nonsense, I certainly did not want to see him again.'

'Come now, Miss Farrer, that simply is not true. A few days later, you were round at Sarah Brown's, trying to get her to arrange a meeting with Alastair Grant. So, you did want to see him. It would help greatly, if you could recollect spending the night of the 25th with Mr Grant.'

'Mr Fothergill, you are asking me to lie for Mr Grant. Why?'

'Not to beat about the bush, Mr Grant has need of an alibi.'

'You want me to testify in a court that Alastair was with me for the whole of the night of the 25 May?'

'That's exactly what we are asking.'

'But, Mr Fothergill, that would be perjury.'

'Please, Miss Farrer, let's not be technical.'

There was a long silence. Arnold Fothergill lit a cigarette while he waited for Lucinda's response.

'I'll tell you what I believe.' There was a new hardness to Lucinda's voice. 'I think that you have told me a pack of lies. What happened on the night of the 25 May which so concerns Alastair? Would that be the night when Yves Richepin was murdered?'

'That is what the French police, in their wisdom, have come to believe.' The lawyer was completely unruffled by Lucinda's attack.

'I believe that Alastair Grant was in some way or other responsible for that crime. I also believe that it was Alastiar who got me grabbed by the "flics" and it was my brother,

151

not bloody Alastair, who pulled the strings to get me out. What have you to say to that, Mr Fothergill?'

'I congratulate you, Miss Farrer. You are a very intelligent and a very perspicacious young lady.' Fothergill smiled at her, like a benign schoolteacher encouraging a promising pupil. 'I assured Alastair that you would not be so gullible as to fall for that line of prattle. So, let's get down to brass tacks. We want you to appear in France as a witness for Alastair.'

'Is Alastair in France, then?'

'No, Miss Farrer, he is still in Britain. But the French have applied for extradition. You see, although the body of the late and unlamented Monsieur Richepin was discovered in Monte Carlo, the presumed scene of the crime is in France and so the case will come before a French court. I must tell you that the case against Alastair is sufficiently strong for the British to be sure to hand him over. It would be better if we got the extradition application quashed, but we cannot pull that off. Alastair's defence must be to produce an alibi when that case comes up in France.'

'Sorry, Mr Fothergill, even if I were prepared to help, there is no way I can get back into France. That was made clear to me when I was thrown out.'

'Ah, but there you are wrong. As a key defence witness, they would be obliged to let you in. Of course, if you were refused admission, that would be even better. No case could stand up against Alastair if we could show that the police were preventing a defence witness from appearing. He'd be let off immediately. No, Miss Farrer, they won't be that stupid. You will be let in.'

'And then?'

'And then, you will tell the court that you and Alastair spent the night of the 25 May together in your London home. They will believe you. The French know that you were lovers and that Alastair spent nights with you at your flat in Paris.'

152

'Since you have admitted that it was not Alastair who got me out of jail in Paris and it was him who got me pulled in, tell me, Mr Fothergill, why should I do this for him?'

'Because, my dear Miss Farrer, the day after your evidence has been given so convincingly, you will find a sum of fifty thousand pounds deposited in a bank account which will have been opened in your name in a bank in Geneva.'

'No.'

'Come now, Miss Farrer, be reasonable. I cannot believe that you have such strong moral scruples.'

'No, Mr Fothergill, I have this sneaking suspicion that the day after I have given my false evidence and got Alastair off the hook, he might forget to pay over the fifty thousand. I could hardly sue him for it, could I?'

'You have my word, Miss Farrer. You'll simply have to trust us.'

'Trust you? I don't know you. Trust Alastair? That's worse: I do know him. No, sir, it's not good enough.'

For the first time, Arnold Fothergill looked rattled and was at a loss for words. It was Lucinda's turn to have a cigarette and she took her time about lighting it and taking a few long draws before continuing.

'Now, dear Mr Fothergill, I realize that you might have a problem with Mr Grant who can be so violent if you do not deliver the goods. So, out of consideration for you, not for him, the bastard, I consent to appear and put out your story.'

Lucinda noted the look of relief on the lawyer's face. She was pleased with herself for the way she had summed up the situation. He started to thank her for changing her mind, but she interrupted.

'No, Mr Fothergull, I have not changed my mind. I shall do what you want, but on my conditions.'

'Which are?'

'A sum of one hundred thousand pounds will be paid into a bank account, in Geneva if you like, but an account in my name, no strings attached, and it will be paid in at least three days before I am called on to appear in court. Understood?'

'But Miss Farrer, once you had the money, we would have no way of ensuring that you keep your side of the bargain.'

'You'll simply have to trust me,' Lucinda replied with a winning smile.

A look of profound misery settled on Arnold Fothergill's features.

'That's a hell of a lot of money to put at risk.'

'Take it or leave it.'

'To use a quasi-legal phrase, you have us by the short and curlies,' he sighed. 'Very well, we do not have any choice.'

'You accept?'

'I accept. I shall be in touch with you shortly to go over the details of your story with you. After all, you will be cross-examined and you must be well rehearsed. I wish you good day, Miss Farrer.'

Lucinda got to her feet and made for the door. As she was about to leave, Arnold Fothergill bade her farewell,

'You are a tough bitch, Miss Farrer.'

'Thank you, Mr Fothergill. From you, I take that as a compliment.'

On the train going back to Hamblewood, the thought which brought a smile to Lucinda's lips was – how the hell could I explain this to Miles.

13

Lucinda waited patiently for her summons from Fothergill. She managed to avoid disclosing to her brother what had taken place at her meeting in London, telling him merely that the solicitor had wanted to clear up some matters with her which related to her tenancy of the flat in Paris. Miles probably did not believe her, but he refrained from challenging her story and Lucinda was grateful for his tact. Her relationship with Miles had become a bit more relaxed and cordial: Lucinda persuaded herself that her righteous brother was just possibly becoming human. When, eventually, Arnold Fothergill asked her to come to London again to go over her story with her, Miles gave her a searching look but limited himself to pleading with her to be careful.

Once again, the venue was the Savoy, Lucinda had to admire Fothergill for his thoroughness and his attention to detail. He handed her a single sheet of paper on which had been typed such information as the clothes which Alastair was supposed to have been wearing when he presented himself at Belgrave Square, the name of the restaurant where they had dined (it was one of those large and completely impersonal establishments where nobody would remember who had eaten there on any particular night) and a precise timetable of their fictitious movements.

'I want you to commit this to memory and then destroy it,' Fothergill told her. 'Now, let's go over your story, point by point. Remember, the prosecution will question you. They will be looking for the slightest inconsistency, so let's get it right, shall we?'

'What's the latest news?' Lucinda asked.

'Well, as you have probably seen in the newspapers, Alastair has appeared in a British court and the judge has ruled that there is a case against him which he will have to answer in a French court. So, he is being extradited, as we knew he would be.'

'Will he have to wait a long time before the trial?'

'No. The case against him had to be virtually completed for presentation here to get extradition, so the prosecution is practically ready to go. We don't want to delay either, so you had better get on with learning your lines.'

The coaching session lasted most of the afternoon. As she

was leaving, Fothergill called to her, 'By the way, Miss Farrer, the French authorities have been informed that you will be appearing as a defence witness and they have indicated that you are free to enter France whenever you please without any objections being raised.'

To Miles, Lucinda mentioned that she would be obliged to go to France in connection with the case against Alastair. She did not think it a good idea to say that she was due to appear as star witness for the defence: Miles would naturally expect her to be helping the prosection against the man who had so recently framed her. Of course, he and everybody else, would know, after she had done her act in the witness box, but it would be too late for them to do anything about it and Lucinda had no intention of returning to England to face the music. Instead, she spent her time considering how she would spend her hundred thousand pounds in settling somewhere more congenial. Perhaps she would buy herself a small villa on the Mediterranean, or maybe it would be a good idea to take off for California, or what about somewhere really remote like Bali or the Seychelles? She could make up her mind when the time came, but meanwhile, she got a great deal of pleasure, in mentally spending the money which she had not yet received.

She was all set to go to France, when Merton phoned.

'I thought that you would like to know, I have heard from Jenny.'

'Is she OK?'

'She's fine. The police did not hold her for long and she says that they did not give her too tough a time.'

'Where is she?'

'She's still in Paris.'

'Really?' Lucinda was surprised. She had thought that if Jennifer was fortunate enough to get out of custody, she would have been bundled off back to England just as had happened to her. 'Actually, I am going back to Paris myself in a few days.'

'Yes, I gathered as much,' Merton replied. 'Please,

Lucinda, do look Jennifer up as soon as you arrive. I'll give you her address. Got a pen handy?'

Lucinda rummaged in her bag and found a ball-point.

'17, Rue Blomet. That's in the 15th, near Grenelle. She has a studio on the third floor, the staircase on the right. There's no phone there yet and I don't know if she intends to stay long enough to have one installed, but do go and see her. She's expecting you.'

'How can she be expecting me: she does not know I am coming to Paris?'

'She has heard. She knows far more than you think. Promise me, Lucinda, you will go there before you do anything else in Paris?'

Lucinda could not remember ever hearing Merton sound so worried and so insistent.

'Yes, of course I'll look her up. Whatever is the matter, Merton?'

'The matter? Nothing, nothing at all.'

For once in his life, Lucinda thought, the great Merton Maxwell was putting on an unconvincing act.

It was a bright, sunny afternoon when Lucinda explored the quiet, unpretentious building on the Rue Blomet. She had checked into a hotel which had been selected by the methodical Arnold Fothergill, an unassuming place off the tourist track. She wanted to do some shopping but she had promised Merton to look up Jennifer before anything else and he had been so urgent that she decided to keep her word despite the temptations of the boutiques.

Jennifer opened the door to her and kissed her long and lovingly. Lucinda noted that she was pale and her face drawn as though she had been under a lot of strain, but the look of suffering made her appear more beautiful than ever in Lucinda's eyes.

'You don't seem very surprised to see me,' Lucinda laughed.

'I'm not. I knew that you would come.'

'Merton made such a big thing of it. I had to see you before I did anything else the moment I arrived in Paris.'

'He was quite right. I must have a serious talk to you, but, first of all, let me look at you, dearest Lucinda.'

It was as though they were back at Hurstmonbury. Jennifer was the adorable goddess whom she had worshipped from afar, once more. But, no longer was she the unapproachable object of desire.

'Oh, Jennifer,' she whispered, 'you have no idea how much I have missed you.'

'I know, Lucinda, darling.'

Jennifer took her into her arms and held her close. Their bodies trembled with emotion.

'It's been so long, Jennifer.'

'Too long, my sweet.'

Jennifer stroked her hair. Her fingers were smooth and sensitive. Lucinda's skin tingled. Their lips met and into that kiss, went a lifetime of passion. All her other loves were but pale reflections of what she felt for Jennifer.

'Let's not stand here,' Jennifer's voice was husky, as she led the way across to the sofa which, by pulling on a couple of handles, was swiftly converted into a bed.

It was Jennifer who took the initiative, gently but firmly removing the clothes from Lucinda's unresisting body.

'Now, you undress me,' Jennifer told her.

Lucinda obeyed and reverently kissed her partner's perfect, white breasts. Jennifer lay her on her back and lowered her own body on top of her. Nothing had changed over the years. Jennifer's scent was the same musky, sweet odour which made her head swim with desire. She buried her head in Jennifer's breast, then tucked it under her armpit where the smell of her was stronger, richer, so much her own personal smell, different from every other body in the world.

Jennifer's hands kneaded and fondled her, taking possession of every part of her. Lucinda felt that overwhelming urge to be part of her lover, to belong to her and be completely possessed by her. She gasped with pleasure, as Jennifer's masterful fingers entered her. She was like a finely tuned musical instrument, made to respond to the touch of her mistress, and how beautifully Jennifer played her until every nerve and muscle of her being strained to be one with that wonderful body which pressed down upon her and which she caressed and kissed feverishly.

'Oh, Jennifer, Jennifer,' she moaned, 'What do we need men for? Just you and me, it's so good.'

Jennifer did not reply, but thrust her down into the bed and raised herself above Lucinda until she grasped her face between her thighs. Lucinda felt herself being drenched by her idol's juices and she sucked and nuzzled, as if she could climb back into Jennifer's womb., She felt Jennifer's muscles tauten, heard her breathing come quicker and quicker. Jennifer was pushing herself into Lucinda's eager mouth, ever harder and with a rhythm which would not be denied, until, with a scream, she collapsed on Lucinda, gasping and throbbing.

Then, it was Lucinda's turn, but it was with her fingers that Jennifer finally drove her to a climax so intense and so uncontrolled that Lucinda felt as if the world around her had dissolved and she, herself, had ceased to exist.

They lay back, panting, spent. Their bodies were numbed with the intensity of their pleasure, but the burning fires within them blazed unabated. They could not bear to drag their bodies apart. Lucinda knew that ever since her schoolgirl fantasies, she had been waiting for this one marvellous fusion of her body with that of Jennifer. All her other lovers, even the earlier times with Jennifer herself, had been no more than a preparation leading up to this triumphant culmination of her sexuality and their physical passion. Jennifer filled every one of her senses, her husky voice murmuring words of endearment in her ear while the vision of her perfect body blotted out the sight of all the everyday things around them. She rejoiced in the tangy odour that was Jennifer and the feeling of her lover's body, her hands, her lips, made her feel giddy. Lucinda was absolutely obsessed by Jennifer and Jennifer responded completely and devotedly to her unquenchable lust.

It would never end. Every time that they stopped, exhausted and drained, the urge drove them to start again. They lost count of how many times they came: each time was better, fuller, more total than the last. And every time, it was Jennifer who led. She was utterly dominant and Lucinda was content to do her bidding. She was completely in the older girl's power, and Jennifer knew it.

'Lucinda, do you really love me?'

'Jennifer! How can you ask such a thing! You know I worship you.'

'Then, my darling, don't fight me.'

'What do you mean? You know that I'd never do anything to hurt you.'

They were lying side by side. Jennifer sat up and looked down at Lucinda. Her expression was serious, yet tender.

'I was very much in love with Yves, you know. Don't ask me why: it was just one of those things. He was not all that handsome and he was a selfish, sadistic lover. I was aware of all his bad points but, somehow they didn't matter. Can you ever explain being in love? And now, he's dead, murdered.'

Jennifer's voice was bitter and her eyes misty with barely suppressed tears. Lucinda waited for her to go on.

'I was his woman and I shall never forgive the swine who killed him. Never. Do you know what it means to crave for vengeance, Lucinda?'

'I can understand how you feel,' Lucinda replied slowly, 'but you know that I had no part in the horrible business.'

'Don't fight me, Lucinda,' Jennifer repeated. 'I shall revenge his death. Alastair Grant is evil, disgusting, and he thinks that he is going to get away with it. But he won't, Lucinda, he'll pay for what he has done, I swear it.'

'Surely you don't believe that Alastair actually killed Yves, himself?'

'Don't play games with me, Lucinda. You know as well as I do that Alastair is as guilty as hell. You must not cover up for him – not if you love me as you say you do.'

A sensation of utter helplessness swept over Lucinda. Jennifer was irresistible: yet how could she extricate herself from the impossible predicament in which she found herself?

'I love you, Lucinda, and I don't want you to get hurt.' Jennifer squeezed her hand. 'I am not supposed to tell you this, but to hell with legal rights and wrongs. You must not appear at the trial of Alastair. You see, there is overwhelming proof of Alastair's guilt in the hands of the police.

'Listen, Lucinda. I was with Yves the evening before he was killed. We had been out together and we went back to Yves' house.'

'You mean his flat in Paris?'

'No, my dear, his house. He had a place not far from Cannes. You knew that he had a house in the country, didn't you?'

'He had mentioned it, but I didn't know where it was.'

'Well, when we got back, there was a message on Yves' telephone answering machine. It was a message from Alastair and it was Alastair's voice on the tape. He asked Yves to meet him that night at a club in Cannes. Yves left for that rendezvous and he never came back.'

'But, Jennifer, I don't understand. Both you and I had been pulled in by the police. Didn't Yves suspect Alastair?'

'He thought that the trouble had been caused by a gang which had been trying to muscle in on his racket. Alastair claimed to have some information that he wanted to discuss with Yves, treacherous bastard that he was.'

'And you mean to tell me that Alastair was stupid enough to leave evidence like the tape in Yves' answering machine?'

'Oh, no, Lucinda my darling, your precious Alastair thought that he had covered his tracks, but he made an important miscalculation. You see, he did not know that I was with Yves. Alastair thought that Yves had come to the south of France, alone. When he never returned from that meeting, I had a feeling that the tape with Alastair's voice on it might be important. So, I took it out of the answering machine and substituted another one.'

'Don't tell me,' Lucinda breathed. 'Somebody broke in and stole the tape?'

Jennifer shook her head.

'No, my love, that would have been too obvious and have aroused suspicion. We had an intruder all right, though he tried to leave no trace. There was an "accidental" fire in the house a couple of days later. Didn't do much damage, but it started in the lounge where the telephone stood. The phone and the answering machine were destroyed. We were supposed to think that it happened by chance but, by that time I was away, and the tape went with me. Now, it is with the police and they have managed to match the voice on the tape with voice-prints of Alastair. It was him all right. He was in France on the 25 May and lured Yves to his death. Now, Lucinda, do you see why you must not swear to an alibi for him in court?'

'So Alastair really was responsible for the murder.' Lucinda spoke slowly and sadly.

'You knew he was.'

'I hoped that there was some other explanation and that he needed an alibi simply because he was under suspicion and could not clear himself.' Lucinda was miserable.

'Be honest, Lucinda, you must have known. Why are you prepared to protect him?'

'Jennifer, I'm frightened.'

Jennifer shook her head.

'No, my sweet, you've done a deal. Alastair has promised to pay you.'

'He's offered me fifty thousand pounds,' Lucinda confessed.

'Yes, Lucinda, but you are expecting a hundred thousand. And, although you don't know it yet, you should be paid at the Union bank of Switzerland in Geneva.'

Lucinda stared at Jennifer in disbelief.

'How do you know all this?' she whispered. 'But, I am frightened. What will Alastair do to me if I don't play ball? You have convinced me that he is a killer.'

'But, don't you see, you've got it all wrong, Lucinda. What do you think will happen to you if you were to get him set free after you have virtually blackmailed him for all that money? Once he is scot free, how long do you think that you would be allowed to walk about before you met with an unfortunate accident? Face it, Lucinda, give that evidence and you will be signing your own death warrant.'

'Jennifer, tell me, how do you know all this?' Lucinda repeated.

Jennifer gave her a reassuring kiss.

'Alastair has quite a gang working for him but one of his pals is a police plant. They know exactly what his plans are and, the moment that you give your false evidence, they are ready to arrest you for perjury – and for being an accessory to murder, for that's what you will be.'

'So, this is why you wanted to see me as soon as I arrived and before I had a chance to talk to anybody else.'

'It was for your own good, Lucinda. Don't you see that?'

Lucinda nodded.

'Tell me something, Jennifer. How is it that you are so much in the confidence of the police?'

'Lucinda, my love, I think that it is time that you met Inspector Leclair, who is in charge of the case. I met him after I had been arrested and we became good friends. Although I was involved with Yves who was usually on the wrong side of the law, I found Leclair very sympathetic. He seems to find me attractive and he can be indiscreet. He is going to get Alastair, whatever you may say in court. And he can protect you, Lucinda, if you àre sensible. What do you say?'

'I think that I ought to meet your kind policeman,' Lucinda answered.

'I am so glad,' Jennifer said, as she kissed Lucinda. 'Leclair will arrange everything, you see. I think that you will like him: I am sure that he will like you.'

Part 5

14

It had been a long, fine autumn and a few russet and golden leaves lingered on the trees but there was a winter chill in the air. Lucinda let herself into the flat on the Avenue Mozart and savoured its welcoming warmth.

'Want a cup of tea,?' Jennifer called from the kitchen. 'I've just made some fresh.'

'Yes, please. I'll put the champagne in the 'fridge and get it nicely chilled.'

'I hope that you got something good.'

'The best.' Lucinda came into the kitchen and displayed proudly a magnum of Dom Perignon. 'We have something to celebrate, so let's do it in style.'

As they carried their cups into the lounge, there was a loud crash from the bedroom, followed by an outburst of laughter.

'Really, Lucinda, you must do something about fixing the headboard of the bed. One day it's going to kill somebody.'

'Doesn't seem to have done any damage to the present occupants,' Lucinda replied with a smile. 'Is that our Sarah dispensing a little hospitality?'

'She has a nice, generous nature,' Jennifer explained.

More sounds emanated from the bedroom, subdued voices and an occasional giggle. Lucinda and Jennifer sipped their tea and chatted. They had long learnt to ignore the offstage noises in the flat whenever Sarah Brown occupied the bedroom and dispensed hospitality.

'Is she with our guardian angel?' Lucinda asked.

'That's right. Quite a regular visitor.'

'I'm glad that he has taken such a fancy to Sarah. It's the best insurance policy we could have.'

Sarah opened the bedroom door and walked into the lounge. Paris had changed her. She had adopted a more sophisticated hair style and her clothes had a light, informal look. As if to stress that informality, Sarah was still zipping up her skirt, as she joined the other girls. Behind her, walked a fresh complexioned man of about forty with iron grey hair and an unexpected black, bristly moustache. He smiled cheerfully at his hostesses.

'Do sit down, dear, dear Inspector,' Lucinda cooed at him. 'We're waiting for my brother, Miles. You met him at the trial, remember? Can you stay for an hour or two?'

'No, I have to be on duty in about an hour's time,' replied Inspector Leclair. 'I can hang on for perhaps twenty minutes, then I will have to go.'

'The champagne should be cold by then. You must have a drink with us.'

They were interrupted by the doorbell. Jennifer jumped to her feet and went and let in Miles.

'I'm so glad that you happened to be in Paris and could spare the time to look in,' said his sister, as she kissed him.

'Well, you made such a fuss about this celebration that you are having. What's it all about, Lucinda?'

'Wait for the bubbly,' she answered and she strode into the kitchen to return a moment later bearing a tray, charged with the champagne and glasses.

She poured out the champagne and handed a glass to everybody.

'I give you a toast.' Lucinda raised her glass. 'Tonight, we drink to Alastair Grant as we bid him farewell for ever.

'Alastair Grant?' cried Miles. 'I wouldn't have thought that you were on such fond terms. What are you talking about?'

'Oh, you have only just arrived from England, so you would not have kept up with our daily scandal over here.' Jennifer smiled at Miles and went on to enlighten him. 'As Lucinda says, it's by way of a final farewell. They cut off his head today.'

'Cut off his head,' Miles echoed.'

'He went to the guillotine, monsieur.' Inspector Leclair was rather more formal.

168

'I thought that the guillotine was being abolished?' Miles remarked.

Leclair replied, 'There is a move to get a law through the National Assembly. I expect that it will become law. Just think, your Mr Grant may have achieved the unenviable distinction of being the last man in France to suffer capital punishment.'

'Poor, old Alastair!' Sarah's tone was not noticeably sympathetic. 'Still, that ought to get him into the Guinness Book of Records.'

'How typical of him,' Lucinda said. 'In death, as in life, Alastair always managed some macabre drama.'

'I say, Lucinda, I think that you show bad taste,' her brother protested, but he sipped his champagne approvingly. 'Is that why you are here, Inspector? I must admit that when I saw you, I was afraid that Lucinda had got into some more trouble.'

'Not at all. We felt that after your sister confessed to the police that Mr Grant had attempted to get her to swear a false alibi for him and he was convicted of murder, partly on her evidence and that of Miss Maxwell, the two of them might have been in some danger from friends of Mr Grant. So, I have been keeping an eye on them and I pass by from time to time to make sure that they are all right.'

'Oh, I see. I thought that there had to be a good reason for your being here,' Miles remarked solemnly.

'There was a very good reason,' Sarah put in. 'There always is a good reason.'

'Tell me, Lucinda, how is it that you still have this apartment? I thought that it belonged to Alastair Grant?'

'No, Miles. It belonged to the company, Entreprises Richegrant. That company was owned by Alastair Grant and Yves Richepin: they are both dead, so we have the flat.'

'No, Lucinda, it's not as simple as that.' Miles was once more the knowledgeable lawyer, ready to explain the intricacies of the business world to his kid sister.

'Oh, it's all right, Miles. We own the company now, Jennifer and I.'

169

'You own Richegrant?' Miles repeated in astonishment.

'Yes, but of course we have changed its name. We took a leaf out of the book of the former proprietors and used our own names. Entreprises Lucifer, what do you think of that?'

'Very appropriate,' murmured her bemused brother. 'But how did you manage to take over a company from a brace of corpses?'

'There are lawyers who specialize in these rather difficult things, like finding documents, all signed and dated some time in the past. Jean-François found the man who did it for us. I don't know what we would have done without Jean-François, he has been so helpful – an absolute angel.'

'Jean-François?'

'That's my name, monsieur,' said Inspector Leclair. Then, he turned to Lucinda and added, 'Please, madame, be a little discreet.'

Lucinda laughed. 'Don't worry, your reputation as a pillar of law and order is safe. Miles is the soul of discretion.'

Leclair smiled nervously at Miles and gulped down the last of his drink.

'I had better be on my way,' he said apologetically. 'I don't want to be late for duty, do I? It's been a pleasure seeing you, Monsieur Farrer. I am sure that you won't find it necessary to mention my presence here or my involvement with these young ladies to anyone.'

He kissed Lucinda and Jennifer lightly on the cheek. His farewell to Sarah was a bit more protracted.

'So,' Miles mused after the Inspector had left, 'you not only have the flat, but all of the business of that company now belongs to you and Jennifer. Just the two of you. Very nice!'

'Well, we are the two disclosed shareholders, but there are two other people who have a slice of the action.'

Miles raised his eyebrows.

'We had to give some part to Sarah,' his sister continued. 'You see, it was thanks to her presence of mind that we have any business at all.'

170

'I was working in the office when Alastair was arrested,' Sarah told him. 'When I first came to Paris, I believed that it was Yves and your sister who had double-crossed Alastair and that he was simply an innocent victim. When Jean-François was put in charge of the case, he showed me how wrong I was. So, when I learnt that the police were going to take everything away from the office, I removed the files with the names of all our clients and the addresses and phone numbers of our employees. You understand, I wanted to keep them safe, so I handed them over to Lucinda.'

'You don't think that the police would have kept them safe?' Miles asked sarcastically.

'I was afraid that they might have kept them too safe.'

'Yes, I see. And I suppose that it was Jean-François who warned you that the police were about to seize the contents of the office.'

'Of course it was,' Jennifer smiled at Miles. 'He is really a dear, sweet policeman and he has been a great help to us in a lot of ways. You see, he is very fond of Sarah. It couldn't have worked out better.'

'Let me guess,' Miles remarked, 'the fourth owner of your Entreprises Lucifer wouldn't happen to be the same, helpful policeman, would it?'

'Oh, Miles, how clever of you! But there is nothing in his name, of course.'

'Of course,' Miles agreed.

They were interrupted by the phone. Lucinda took the call in the bedroom but soon returned.

'It was Babette,' she announced to Jennifer and Sarah. 'Calling from Cannes. No trouble. In fact, she's been doing rather well and she's sending in some money on Monday.'

'How that girl has improved, once she got out of that office,' Jennifer commented. 'She used to be one great pain in the arse.'

'She just needed to get out into the field,' Lucinda replied.

'I know it's none of my business,' Miles said, 'but is Babette the girl who gave evidence during the trial?'

They nodded.

'Well, I may not be much of a judge, but I would have thought that she was far too plain for the sort of work that I have realized your company goes in for. Very plain and pimply, if I remember correctly. Not at all a pretty face. I must say, I would not fancy looking at her while I was indulging in love-making.'

'Very delicately put, Miles,' Lucinda smiled her approval, 'but, you see, Babette specializes in providing our clients with a service which is much appreciated and during which they are not able to see her face.'

Miles gave her an enquiring look and Lucinda licked her lips expressively. Miles blushed and changed the subject.

'Well, you seem to be doing very well here, judging by the way you are living it up. Trade's pretty brisk, eh?'

'Mustn't grumble, but we were fortunate in that I managed to lay my hands on quite a tidy bit of working capital before we went fully into operation.'

Lucinda made the statement sound casual but her brother was not fooled.

'Would that happen to be a sum of a hundred thousand pounds which somehow came your way?'

'Who told you about that?'

'Don't look so shocked, Lucinda. When you were at home, you asked me about a certain Mr Arnold Fothergill. I am sure that you have not forgotten. There had to be a reason for your interest in that somewhat shady character, so I was not completely unprepared when he turned up at my chambers and wanted to know if I could put him in touch with you. It seems that during some financial transactions, he had, by mistake, transferred a considerable sum of money to your account, by mistake – or so he said. He was certain that, once you realized the error, you would be willing to return the funds. He did not want to go into any details with me but I insisted that I had to know a lot more before talking to you. Very reluctantly, he disclosed the figure of a hundred thousand pounds and admitted that the money belonged to Alastair Grant.'

'What did you tell him? You didn't promise him that you would get the money back for him, did you, Miles?'

'Don't get excited, Lucinda,' Miles said soothingly, 'I have no love for Mr Arnold Fothergull, nor for that matter for the late Mr Alastair Grant. I told that legal luminary that I was sure that you were fully entitled to any money which happened to be in your account. Probably, you had performed some service for Mr Grant of which the worthy Fothergill was unaware and I did not think that I ought to get involved. I advised him, if he felt that you were not entitled to the money to take the matter to the courts.'

'Is there anything that he can do to get at us?' Sarah asked.

'Nothing legal,' Miles replied. 'The British courts would do nothing about something which took place completely outside the country and was illegal anyway. The Swiss bank which handled the money would not want to know. The only danger was that he would get some tough types to come and rough you up, but your understanding French policeman is obviously covering that angle. And now, with the final disappearance of Alastair Grant, I would expect that Fothergill will lose interest in the matter. Without Grant, his case collapses and he has nothing to gain in persevering against you. And I left him in no doubt that if he tried anything in England, he would have me to reckon with and I could cause a lot of trouble for him.'

'Good, old Miles,' Lucinda laughed, 'spoken like a true brother. My, how you have improved! Have some more champagne.'

After several more glasses, Miles was mildly tipsy. He grinned benignly at his sister and the other two girls.

'I must confess,' he told them, 'that I used to be perhaps a trifle too strict. Mind you, Lucinda got up to every kind of mischief and I felt responsible for her since our parents didn't give a damn. But maybe I was a bit too solemn and too conventional. After all, you kids don't seem to be doing anyone any harm.'

His eyes were brimming with tears of loving kindness.

'You've been a real sport, the way you helped getting me

out of jail and during and after the trial. And I am so glad that you settled bloody, old Fothergill. I think that we ought to show our gratitude in some tangible form. Don't you girls agree?' Lucinda demanded of her partners.

'That's OK.' Miles protested. 'I don't want to be paid: I enjoyed doing what I did.'

'I never mentioned money,' his sister patted his hand reassuringly. 'No, we the proprietors of Entreprises Lucifer would like to present you with a free sample of our wares, as a token of our esteem and gratitude. I would like to propose that as a motion to my board.'

'Seconded,' said Jennifer.

'Carried unanimously,' said Sarah.

'You mean that you are offering me one of your girls?' His tone was incredulous.

'That's right,' Lucinda told him. 'However, to keep things simple, we would be obliged if you would confine your choice to one of the executives who are presently here. I mean, it would be an awful waste of effort to bring in Babette, for example from Cannes, for a quick blow job.'

'What, take one of you three?'

'That's right, Miles, you show a sure grasp of the situation. Now, what do you say: I assure you that all three of us are highly qualified experts. What you are being offered, my lad, is the top of the market, the cream of the cream!'

'Well, I mean to say,' Miles mumbled in acute embarrassment under the provocative scrutiny of the three attractive young women. 'I can't touch you, Lucinda. That would be incest.'

'Suit yourself, my dear. You might find it more of a turn on.'

Miles shook his head.

'And as for Miss Brown, she has only just emerged from a session with Jean-François. You must be tired.'

But there was a smouldering desire in his eye as he spoke, as if he wanted her to contradict him.

'I think that we have discovered your brother's true

174

preference,' Jennifer murmured to Lucinda.

'Do you fancy me?' Sarah spoke demurely but she stretched her body invitingly and Miles could not take his eyes off her.

'Oh, yes. I could really go for you.'

'Well, Miles dear, let's not trouble the other two.'

'You know, nothing like this has ever happened to me before,' Miles admitted shyly to his sister.

'Good for you! Perhaps your luck is changing,' Jennifer encouraged him.

'For goodness sake, get on with it,' snapped Lucinda, 'anybody would think that you were still a virgin.'

Miles still hesitated and his cheeks glowed crimson.

'Come along,' said Sarah, taking him by the hand, 'and don't be bothered by the idea that Jean-François would have worn me out: he's just put me in the mood. Tell me, wouldn't you rather drive a car that's been warmed up than one with an engine that is still stone cold?'

'Are you sure that you don't mind?' Miles asked, as he let himself be steered into the bedroom. 'I am afraid I am not very experienced.'

'Do you know, I honestly think that it is his first time,' Lucinda said wonderingly to Jennifer.

'Don't let it upset you,' Jennifer laughed, 'there's a first time for everybody. Well, nearly everybody. I don't suppose you can still remember yours, but you should have found the time to take your brother in hand and done something about his education. Sarah will take good care of him. He could not have found anybody nicer to deflower him.'

The bedroom door closed and the two girls grinned at each other and strained their ears. They could hear muffled voices, his apologetic and hers encouraging.

'Relax, Lucinda, he'll get there even if Sarah has to give him a map and compass.'

The voices were silent. Lucinda was delighted to make out the faint squeaks and creaks of the bed.

'Attaboy, Miles,' she whispered.

Jennifer put her arms around her and pressed her lips to the sweetness of Lucinda's mouth. Once again, she asked, 'I love you so, Lucinda: who needs men?'

'They do come in useful in our line of business,' Lucinda reminded her. 'And, although I love you too, dearest Jennifer, I do need the feel of a man sometimes as well. I believe you do too, but you have not yet got over Yves. Wait and see.'

Their reverie was shattered by a deafening crash.

'Oh, God, the headboard. That's probably put Miles off sex for the rest of his life!'

15

Miles survived the collapse of the bed and Entreprises Lucifer continued to provide much appreciated services for its clientele and to flourish. The three women and their sympathetic policeman were a harmonious team. They enjoyed their life and work together but there was an inner restlessness which occasionally nagged at Lucinda. She said nothing to the others but she knew that the day would come when she would want to move on to something new.

They were eating their breakfast one morning and Jennifer was reading a newspaper.

'You know what?' she called out. 'This new government of Mitterand has done what it promised. They have abolished the death penalty. Just think, if Alastair could only have waited a few months, he would still be alive. However, he did achieve the distinction of being the last man to be executed in France.'

'I don't suppose that would have been much of a comfort to him, even if he had known it before he lost his head,' Sarah commented.

But it was Lucinda who passed the final judgement on the man she had hated yet had slept with, who had betrayed her and had been betrayed by her.

'How typical of Alastair! He always came too soon.'